I Would Have

Saved Them If

I Could

Leonard Michaels

NEW YORK

I Would Have

Saved Them If

I Could

Farrar, Straus & Giroux

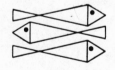

For Leon and Anna Michaels

CONTENTS

Murderers

1ァ

WHEN MY UNCLE Moe dropped dead of a heart attack I became expert in the subway system. With a nickel I'd get to Queens, twist and zoom to Coney Island, twist again toward the George Washington Bridge—beyond which was darkness. I wanted proximity to darkness, strangeness. Who doesn't? The poor in spirit, the ignorant and frightened. My family came from Poland, then never went any place until they had heart attacks. The consummation of years in one neighborhood: a black Cadillac, corpse inside. We should have buried Uncle Moe where he shuffled away his life, in the kitchen or toilet, under the linoleum, near the coffee pot. Anyhow, they were dropping on Henry Street and Cherry Street. Blue lips. The previous winter it was cousin Charlie, forty-five years old. Moe, Charlie, Sam, Adele—family meant a punch in the chest, fire in the arm. I didn't want to wait for it. I went to Harlem, the Polo Grounds, Far Rockaway, thousands of miles on nickels, mainly underground. Tenements watched me go, day after day, fingering nickels. One afternoon I stopped to grind my heel against the curb. Melvin and Arnold Bloom appeared, then Harold Cohen. Melvin said, "You step in dog shit?" Grinding was my answer. Harold Cohen said, "The rabbi is home. I saw him on Market Street. He was walking fast." Oily Arnold, eleven years old, began to urge: "Let's go up to our roof." The decision waited for me. I considered the roof, the view of industrial Brooklyn, the Battery, ships in the river, bridges, towers, and the rabbi's apartment. "All right," I said. We didn't giggle or look to one another for moral signals. We were running.

The blinds were up and curtains pulled, giving sunlight, wind, birds to the rabbi's apartment—a magnificent metropolitan view. The rabbi and his wife never took it, but in the light and air of summer afternoons, in the eye of gull and pigeon, they were joyous. A bearded young man, and his young pink wife, sacramentally bald. Beard and Baldy, with everything to see, looked at each other. From a water tank on the opposite roof, higher than their windows, we looked at them. In psychoanalysis this is "The Primal Scene." To achieve the primal scene we crossed a ledge six inches wide. A half-inch indentation in the brick gave us fingerholds. We dragged bellies and groins against the brick face to a steel ladder. It went up the side of the building, bolted into brick, and up the side of the water tank to a slanted tin roof which caught the afternoon sun. We sat on that roof like angels, shot through with light, derealized in brilliance. Our sneakers sucked hot slanted metal. Palms and fingers pressed to bone on nailheads.

The Brooklyn Navy Yard with destroyers and aircraft carriers, the Statue of Liberty putting the sky to the torch, the dull remote skyscrapers of Wall Street, and the Empire State Building were among the wonders we dominated. Our view of the holy man and his wife, on their living-room couch and floor, on the bed in their bedroom, could not be improved. Unless we got closer. But fifty feet across the air was right. We heard their phonograph and watched them dancing. We couldn't hear the gratifications or see pimples. We smelled nothing. We didn't want to touch.

For a while I watched them. Then I gazed beyond into shimmering nullity, gray, blue, and green murmuring over rooftops and towers. I had watched them before. I could tantalize myself with this brief ocular perversion, the general cleansing nihil of a view. This was the beginning of philosophy. I indulged in ambience, in space like eons. So what if my uncle Moe was dead? I was philosophical and luxurious. I didn't even have to look at the rabbi and his wife. After all, how many times had we dissolved stickball games when the rabbi came home? How many times had we risked shameful discovery, scrambling up the ladder, exposed to their windows—if they looked. We risked life itself to achieve this eminence. I looked at the rabbi and his wife.

Today she was a blonde. Bald didn't mean no wigs. She had ten wigs, ten colors, fifty styles. She looked different, the same, and very good. A human theme in which nothing begat anything and was gorgeous. To me she was the world's lesson. Aryan yellow slipped through pins about her ears. An olive complexion mediated yellow hair and Arabic black eyes. Could one care what she really looked like? What was *really*? The minute you wondered, she looked like something else, in another wig, another style. Without the wigs she was a baldy-bean lady. Today she was a blonde. Not blonde. *A* blonde. The phonograph blared and her deep loops flowed Tommy Dorsey, Benny Goodman, and then the thing itself, Choo-Choo Lopez. Rumba! One, two-three. One, two-three. The rabbi stepped away to delight in blond imagination. Twirling and individual, he stepped away snapping fingers, going high and light on his toes. A short bearded man, balls afling, cock shuddering like a springboard. Rumba! One, two-three. *Olé! Vaya,* Choo-Choo!

I was on my way to spend some time in Cuba.
Stopped off at Miami Beach, la-la.
Oh, what a rumba they teach, la-la.
Way down in Miami Beach,
Oh, what a chroombah they teach, la-la.
Way-down-in-Miami-Beach.

She, on the other hand, was somewhat reserved. A shift in one lush hip was total rumba. He was Mr. Life. She was dancing. He was a naked man. She was what she was in the garment of her soft, essential self. He was snapping, clapping, hopping to the beat. The beat lived in her visible music, her lovely self. Except for the wig. Also a watchband that desecrated her wrist. But it gave her a bit of the whorish. She never took it off.

Harold Cohen began a cocktail-mixer motion, masturbating with two fists. Seeing him at such hard futile work, braced only by sneakers, was terrifying. But I grinned. Out of terror, I twisted an encouraging face. Melvin Bloom kept one hand on the tin. The other knuckled the rumba numbers into the back of my head. Nodding like a defective, little Arnold Bloom chewed his lip and squealed as the rabbi and his wife smacked together. The rabbi clapped her buttocks, fingers buried in the cleft. They stood only on his legs. His back arched, knees bent, thighs thick with thrust, up, up, up. Her legs wrapped his hips, ankles crossed, hooked for con-striction. "Oi, oi, oi," she cried, wig flashing left, right, tossing the Brooklyn Navy Yard, the Statue of Liberty, and the Empire State Building to hell. Arnold squealed oi, squealing rubber. His sneaker heels stabbed tin to stop his slide. Melvin said, "Idiot." Arnold's ring hooked a nailhead and the ring and ring finger remained. The hand, the arm, the rest of him, were gone.

We rumbled down the ladder. "Oi, oi, oi," she yelled. In a freak of ecstasy her eyes had rolled and caught us. The rabbi drilled to her quick and she had us. "*OI, OI,*" she yelled above congas going clop, doom-doom, clop, doom-doom on the way to Cuba. The rabbi flew to the window, a red mouth opening in his beard: "Murderers." He couldn't know what he said. Melvin Bloom was crying. My fingers were tearing, bleeding into brick. Harold Cohen, like an adding machine, gibbered the name of God. We moved down the ledge quickly as we dared. Bongos went tocka-ti-tocka, tocka-ti-tocka. The rabbi screamed, "MELVIN BLOOM, PHILLIP LIEBOWITZ, HAROLD COHEN, MELVIN BLOOM," as if our names, screamed this way, naming us where we hung, smashed us into brick.

Nothing was discussed.

The rabbi used his connections, arrangements were made. We were sent to a camp in New Jersey. We hiked and played volleyball. One day, apropos of nothing, Melvin came to me and said little Arnold had been made of gold and he, Melvin, of shit. I appreciated the sentiment, but to my mind they were both made of shit. Harold Cohen never again spoke to either of us. The counselors in the camp were World War II veterans, introspective men. Some carried shrapnel in their bodies. One had a metal plate in his head. Whatever you said to them they seemed to be thinking of something else, even when they answered. But step out of line and a plastic lanyard whistled burning notice across your ass.

At night, lying in the bunkhouse, I listened to owls. I'd never before heard that sound, the sound of darkness, blooming, opening inside you like a mouth.

It like shit except for what happens in that bedroom — and that they murder!

Eating Out

Basketball Player

I WAS THE MOST dedicated basketball player. I don't say the best. In my mind I was terrifically good. In fact I was simply the most dedicated basketball player in the world. I say this because I played continuously, from the time I discovered the meaning of the game at the age of ten, until my mid-twenties. I played outdoors on cement, indoors on wood. I played in heat, wind, and rain. I played in chilly gymnasiums. Walking home I played some more. I played during dinner, in my sleep, in movies, in automobiles and buses, and at stool. I played for over a decade, taking every conceivable shot, with either hand, from every direction. Masses cheered my performance. No intermission, no food, no other human concern, year after year they cheered me on. In living rooms, subways, movies, and schoolyards I heard them. During actual basketball games I also played basketball. I played games within games. When I lost my virginity I eluded my opponent and sank a running hook. Masses saw it happen. I lost my virginity and my girl lost hers. The game had been won. I pulled up my trousers. She snapped her garter belt. I took a jump shot from the corner and another game was underway. I scored in a blind drive from the foul line. We kissed good night. The effect was epileptic. Masses thrashed in their seats, loud holes in their faces. I acknowledged with an automatic nod and hurried down the street, dribbling. A fall-away jumper from the top of the key. It hung in the air. Then, as if sucked down suddenly, it zipped through the hoop. Despite the speed and angle of my shots, I never missed.

Pleasure

MY MOTHER was taking me to the movies. We were walking fast. I didn't know what movie it would be. Neither did my mother. She couldn't read. We were defenseless people. I was ten years old. My mother was five foot nothing. We walked with fast little steps, hands in our pockets, faces down. The school week had ended. I was five days closer to the M.D. My reward for good grades was a movie—black, brilliant pleasure. Encouragement to persist. We walked in a filthy, freezing, blazing wind for half a mile. The pleasure I'll never forget. A girl is struck by a speeding car. A beautiful girl who speaks first-class English—but she is struck down. Blinded, broken, paralyzed. The driver of the car is a handsome doctor. My mother whispers, "Na," the Polish word that stimulates free-associational capacities in children. Mind-spring, this to that. The doctor operates on the girl in a theater of lights, masks, and knives. She has no choice in this matter. Blind and broken. Paralyzed. Lucky for her, she recovers. Her feeling of recovery is thrilling love for the doctor. He has this feeling, too. It spreads from them to everywhere, like the hot, vibrant, glowing moo of a tremendous cow, liquefying distinctions. The world is feeling. Feeling is the deadly car, the broken girl and blinding doctor, the masks, knives, and kisses. Finally there is a sunset. It returns me with smeared and glistening cheeks to the blazing wind. I glance at my mother. She whispers, "Na?" Intelligence springs through my mind like a monkey, seizing the bars, shaking them. We walk fast, with little steps, our hands in our pockets; but my face is lifted to the wind. It shrieks, "Emmmmmdeee." My call.

Leonard Michaels

Something Evil

I SAID, "Ikstein stands outside the door for a
long time before he knocks. Did you suspect that?
Did you suspect that he stands there listening to
what we say before he knocks?" She said, "Did you
know you're crazy?" I said, "I'm not crazy. The
expression on his face, when I open the door, is
giddy and squirmy. As if he'd been doing something
evil, like listening outside our door before he
knocked." She said, "That's Ikstein's expression.
Why do you invite him here? Leave the door open.
He won't be able to listen to us. You won't make
yourself crazy imagining it." I said, "Brilliant, but
he isn't due for an hour and I won't sit here with
the door open." She said, "I hate to listen to you talk
this way. I won't be involved in your lunatic friend-
ships." She opened the door. Ikstein stood there,
giddy and squirmy.

Answers

I BEGAN two hundred hours of continuous reading in the twelve hours that remained before examinations. Melvin Bloom, my roommate, flipped the pages of his textbook in a sweet continuous trance. Reviewing the term's work was his pleasure. He went to sleep early. While he slept I bent into the night, reading, eating Benzedrine, smoking cigarettes. Shrieking dwarfs charged across my notes. Crabs asked me questions. Melvin flipped a page, blinked, flipped another. He effected the same flipping and blinking, with no textbook, during examinations. For every question, answers marched down his optical nerve, neck, arm, and out onto his paper where they stopped in impeccable parade. I'd look at my paper, oily, scratched by ratlike misery, and I'd think of Melvin Bloom. I would think, Oh God, what is going to happen to me.

Leonard Michaels

Mackerel

SHE DIDN'T WANT to move in because there had been a rape on the third floor. I said, "The guy was a wounded veteran, under observation at Bellevue. We'll live on the fifth floor." It was a Victorian office building, converted to apartments. Seven stories, skinny, gray, filigreed face. No elevators. We climbed an iron stairway. "Wounded veteran," I said. "Predictable." My voice echoed in dingy halls. Linoleum cracked as we walked. Beneath the linoleum was older, drier linoleum. The apartments had wooden office doors with smoked-glass windows. The hall toilets were padlocked; through gaps we could see the bowl, overhead tank, bare bulb dangling. "That stairway is good for the heart and legs," I said. She said, "Disgusting, dangerous building." I said, "You do smell piss in the halls and there has been a rape. The janitor admitted it. But people live here, couples, singles, every sex and race. Irish, Italian, Puerto Rican families. Kids run up and down the stairway. A mackerel-crowded iron stream. Radios, TV's, whining day and night.

Not only a piss smell, but pasta, peppers, incense, marijuana. The building is full of life. It's life. Close to the subways, restaurants, movies." She said, "Rapes." I said, "One rape. A wounded man with a steel plate in his head, embittered, driven by undifferentiated needs. The rent is forty dollars a month. To find this place, you understand, I appealed to strangers. From aluminum phone booths, baby, I dialed with ice-blue fingers. It's January in Manhattan. Howling winds come from the rivers." "The rape," she said. I said, "A special and extremely peculiar case. Be logical." Before we finished unpacking, the janitor was stabbed in the head. I said, "A junkie did it. A natural force, a hurricane." She said, "Something is wrong with you. I always felt it instinctively." I said, "I believe I'm not perfect. What do you think is wrong with me?" She said, "It makes me miserable." I said, "No matter how miserable it makes you, say it." She said, "It embarrasses me." I said, "Even if it embarrasses you, say it, be frank. This is America. I'll write it down. Maybe we can sell it and move to a better place." She said, "There's too much." I said, "I'll make a list. Go ahead, leave out nothing. I have a pencil." She said, "Then what?" I said, "Then I'll go to a psychiatrist." She said, "You'll give a distorted account." I said, "I'll make an exact, complete list. See this pencil. It's for making lists. Tell me what to write." She said, "No use." I said, "A junkie did it. Listen to me, bitch, a junkie did it."

Eating Out

FOUR MEN were at the table next to mine. Their collars were open, their ties loose, and their jackets hung on the wall. One man poured dressing on the salad, another tossed the leaves. Another filled the plates and served. One tore bread, another poured wine, another ladled soup. The table was small and square. The men were cramped, but efficient nonetheless, apparently practiced at eating here, this way, hunched over food, heads striking to suck at spoons, tear at forks, then pulling back into studious, invincible mastication. Their lower faces slid and chopped; they didn't talk once. All their eyes, like birds on a wire, perched on a horizontal line above the action. Swallowing muscles flickered in jaws and necks. Had I touched a shoulder and asked for the time, there would have been snarling, a flash of teeth.

What's New

MY MOTHER SAID, "So? What's new?" I said, "Something happened." She said, "I knew it. I had a feeling. I could tell. Why did I ask? Sure, something happened. Why couldn't I sit still? Did I have to ask? I had a feeling. I knew, I knew. What happened?"

The Burglar

I DIALED. The burglar answered and said Ikstein wasn't home. I said tell him I called. The burglar laughed. I said, "What's funny?" The burglar said, "This is a coincidence. When you called I was reading a passage in Ikstein's diary which is about you." I said, "Tell me what it says." The burglar snorted, "Your request is compromising. Just hearing it is compromising." I said, "I'm in the apartment below Ikstein's. We can easily meet and have a little talk about my request. I'll bring something to drink. Do you like marijuana? I know where Ikstein hides his marijuana. I have money with me, also a TV set and a Japanese camera. It's no trouble for me to carry everything up there. One trip." He said if I came upstairs he would kill me.

Like Irony

HE PRIED ME OPEN and disappeared inside, made me urinate, defecate, and screech, then slapped my dossier shut, stuck it in his cabinet, slammed drawer, swallowed key. "Well," he said, "how have you been?" I said, "Actually, that's what I'm here to find out." He said, "People have feelings. They do their best. Some of us say things to people —such as you—in a way that is like irony, but it isn't irony. It's good breeding, manners, tact—we have delicate intentions." I apologized. "So," he said, "tell me your plans." I said, "Now that I know?" "That's right," he said, "I'm delighted that you aren't very stupid."

One Thing

IKSTEIN PLAYED harpsichord music on the phonograph and opened a bottle of wine. I said, "Let's be frank, Ikstein. There's too much crap in this world." He said, "Sure." The harpsichord was raving ravished Bach. Windows were open. The breeze smelled of reasons to live. I told him I didn't care for love. Only women, only their bodies. Talk, dance, conversation—I could do it—but I cared about one thing only. When it was finished, I had to go. Anyhow, I said, generally speaking, women can't stand themselves. Generally speaking, I thought they were right. "How about you, Ikstein?" He made a pleased mouth and said, "I love women, the way they look, talk, dress, and think. I love their hips, necks, breasts, and ankles. But I hate cunts." He stamped the floor. I raised my glass. He raised his. "To life," I said.

this is pretty characteristic of the attitude toward women in V.M. would he agree and does he see this as a limitation in his writing.

Male

SHE WAS ASLEEP. I wondered if I ought to read a newspaper. Nobody phoned. I wanted to run around the block until I dropped dead, but I was afraid of the muggers. I picked up the phone, dialed Ikstein, decided to hang up, but he answered: "This is Ikstein." I said, "Can I come up?" He said nothing. I said, "Ikstein, it's very late, but I can hear your TV." He said, "When I turn it off, I'll throw you out." I grabbed my cigarettes. His door was open. He didn't say hello. We watched a movie, drank beer, smoked. Side by side, hissing gases, insular and simpatico. It was male. I farted. He scratched his scalp, belched, tipped back in his chair with his legs forked out. His bathrobe fell apart, showing the vascular stump. It became a shivering mushroom, then a moon tree waving in the milky flicker. He said, "Well, look who wants to watch the movie." I said, "Hang a shoe on it." He refolded his robe and flicked off the TV. "If you decide to come out," he said, "let me be the first to know. Now go away." I went downstairs, sat on the bed, and put my hand on her belly. She whimpered, belly falling under my palm. She was asleep. I felt like a crazy man.

Dixie

"RICHARD IKSTEIN" was printed on his mailbox. His nighttime visitors called him "Dixie." In every accent, American and foreign, sometimes laughing, sometimes grim. When he fell our ceiling shuddered. Flakes of paint drifted down onto our bed. She hugged me and tried to make conversation: "They're the last romantics." He was pleading for help. "If you like romance so much," I said, "why don't you become a whore." I twisted away, snapped on the radio, found a voice, and made it loud enough to interfere with his pleading. We couldn't hear his words, only sobs and whimpers. By the time he stopped falling, our bed was gritty with paint and plaster dust. We were too tired to get up and slap the sheets clean. In the morning I saw blood on our pillows. "It's on your face too," she said. "You slept on your back." I was for liberation of every kind, but I dressed in silent, tight-ass fury

The friend
Ikstein is
beaten to death

and ran upstairs. "Look at my face, Ikstein," I
shouted, banging at his door. It opened. The police
were dragging him to a stretcher. I showed them
my stained ceiling and bloody pillows. Obvious, but
I had to explain. I told them about Ikstein's visitors,
how he pleaded and sobbed. The police took notes.
She cried when they left. She cried all morning.
"The state is the greatest human achievement," I
said. "Hegel is right. The state is the only human
achievement." She said, "If you like the state so
much, why don't you become a cop."

Crabs

MY MOTHER didn't mention the way things
looked and said there was going to be a bar mitzvah. If I came to it, the relatives "could see" and I
could meet her old friends from Miami. Their
daughter was a college graduate, beautiful, money
up the sunny gazoo. Moreover, it was a double-rabbi
affair, one for the Hebrew, one for English. "Very
classy," she said. I had been to such affairs. A paragraph of Hebrew is followed by a paragraph of

English. The Hebrew sounds like an interruption. Like jungle talk. I hated the organ music, the hidden choirs, the opulent halls. Besides, I had the crabs. I wasn't in the mood for a Miami bitch who probably had gonorrhea. I said, "No." She said, "Where are your values?"

Smile

IN MEMORIAM I recalled his smile, speedy and horizontal, the corners fleeing one another as if to meet in the back of his head. It suggested pain, great difficulties, failure, gleaming life rot. A smile of "Nevertheless." Sometimes we met on the stairs. He'd smile, yet seem to want to dash the other way, slide into the wall, creep by with no hello. But he smiled. "Nevertheless," he smiled. I would try to seem calm, innocuous, nearly dead. That made him more nevertheless. I would tell him something unfortunate about myself—how I'd overdrawn my checking account, lost my wallet, discovered a boil on my balls—and I would laugh at his self-consciously self-conscious, funny remarks. He nodded gratefully, but he didn't believe I thought he was funny. He didn't believe he was funny. I thought about the murder of complex persons. I thought about his smile, bleeding, beaten to death.

Right Number

A GIRL LIVED in the apartment below. We became friends. I'd go there any time, early or late. She opened the door and didn't turn on the light. I undressed in darkness, slid in beside her, made a spoon, and she slid into my spoon. She had no work, nothing she had to do, no one expected her to be any place. Money came to her in the mail. She had a body like Goya's whore and a Botticelli face. She was tall, pale, blond, and wavy. I knocked, she let me in. No questions. We talked fast and moved about from bed to chairs to floor. Sometimes I'd pinch her thigh. Once she knocked a coffee cup into my lap. Finally we had sexual intercourse. We made a lot of jokes and she was on her back. I tried to be gentle. She thrashed in a complimentary way and moaned. Later she said to guess how many men she'd had. I said ten. She said fifteen. How does that sound? It sounds more depraved than I feel. After the Turk, she understood the Ottoman Empire. She said people thought of her as manic-depressive. But it wasn't true. She had good reasons for what she feels. Germans are friskier than you'd imagine. The right number is seven or eight. It sounds like a lot, yet it isn't depraved. It's believable. A girl shouldn't say seven or eight, then describe twenty. What if I said more than ten, less than twenty? How does that sound? Six came in one weekend. They count as one. How old do you think I am? Twenty-eight? I'm only twenty-two. With A, it is a way of making something out of nothing. With B, it is a form of conversation. With C, it is letting him believe something about himself. With D, it is a mistake. I've had seventeen. People think I've had fifty or a hundred. Do I want fifty or a hundred? No. I want twenty-five. Twenty-five or thirty. Do you remember what my face is like? I think it looks sluttish. Indians are the nicest. Blacks don't talk to you afterward. I was raped when I was a kid. Then I rode my bicycle around and around the block and talked to myself in a loud voice. All my life I've tried to keep things from getting out of hand, but I get out of hand. Nothing works. Nothing works. I like you very very much, I said, let's try again. I was gentle. She thrashed in a complimentary way and moaned. The next day she knocked at my door, wearing a handsome gray wool suit and high heels. Her hair had been washed and combed into a style. She looked neat, intelligent, and extremely beautiful. She said she was going to a job interview to have something to do. We hugged for good luck and kissed. Somehow she was on her back. We had sexual intercourse. I wasn't gentle. She whipped in the pelvis and screamed murder. Me too.

Animals

HER SKIN was made of animals, exceedingly tiny, compressed like a billion paps in a breathing sponge. Caressing her, my palm was caressed by the smooth resilient motion in her skin. Awake or asleep, angry, bored, loving, made no difference. Her skin was superior to attitudes or words. It implied the most beautiful girl. And the core of my pleasure ached for her, the one she implied.

God

MY MOTHER SAID, "What's new?" I said, "Nothing." She said, "What? You can tell me. Tell me what's new." I said, "Something happened." She said, "I had a feeling. I could tell. What happened?" I said, "Nothing happened." She said, "Thank God."

the Jewish mother makes a token appearance.

His Certain Way

IKSTEIN HAD A CERTAIN WAY of picking up a spoon, asking for the time, getting down the street from here to there. He would pick up his spoon in his certain way, stick it in the soup, lift it to his mouth, stop, then whisper, "Eat, eat, little Ikily." Everything he did was in his certain way. He

These are like random entries from p 5 journal. what holds it together and why called "Eating Out"

made an impression of making an impression. I remembered it. I remembered Ikstein. It was no different to remember than to see the living Ikstein, in his certain little ways. For me, he never died. He lived where he always lived, in my impression of Ikstein. I could bring him back any time, essentially, for me. "Eat, eat, little Ikily." When he did his work—he was a book and movie reviewer—he always made himself a "nice" bowl of soup. It sat beside his typewriter. He typed a sentence, stopped, said, "Now I'll have a tasty sip of soup." Essentially, for me, Ikstein had no other life. If he had in fact another life, it was never available for me. I could not pretend to regret it was no longer available for him. "Oh, poor Ikstein" would mean "Oh, poor me, what I have lost. The sights and sound of Ikstein." I lost nothing. His loss, I couldn't appreciate. Neither could he. So I remembered Ikstein and felt no sorrow. I mentioned somebody who had married for the second time. "His second wife looks like the first," I said. "As if he were pursuing something." In his certain way, Ikstein said, "Or as if it were pursuing him." Thus, even his mind lived. I said, "My intention was modest, a bit of chitchat, a germ of sense. I wasn't hoping, when I have a headache and feel sick and unable to think, to illuminate the depths. Must you be such a prick, Ikstein?"

Mournful Girls

BUSY NAKED HEELS, a rush of silky things, elastic snaps, clicks, a rattle of beads, hangers clinking, humming, her quick consistent breathing as the mattress dipped. Lips touched mine. Paper cracked flat near my head. Wooden heel shafts knocked in the hallway. I opened my eyes. A ten-dollar bill lay on the pillow. I got up, dressed, stuck the bill in my pocket, went to the apartment below, and asked, "Do you want anything?" She said no. She lay on the bed. On the way back I picked up her mail. "Some letters," I said and dropped them beside her. She lay on the bed, skirt twisted about her hips and belly, blouse open, bra unhooked to ease the spill. Her blanket was smooth. I whispered, "Mona, Melanie, Mildred, Sarah, Nora, Dora, Sadie." She whispered, "Mournful girls." I lost the beginning of the next sentence before I heard the end. She heard as much, glanced at me, quit talking. We undressed. I tugged her off the bed to the mirror. I looked at her. She looked at me. Our arms slipped around them. All had sexual intercourse. I was upstairs when she returned from work. She asked, "Why didn't you go to the grocery?" I said, "It will take five minutes," and dashed out. The street was dark, figures appeared and jerked by. In the grocery I couldn't find the ten-dollar bill. It wasn't in my pockets. It wasn't on the floor. I ran back along the street, neck bent like a dog's, inspecting the flux of cigarette butts, candy wrappers, spittle plops, dog piss, beer cans, broken glass, granular pavement—then remembered—and ran upstairs quietly. She lay on the bed. The milk and meat were warm, butter loose and greasy. Everything except the cream cheese was in the bag beside her bed. She lay on the bed, gnawing cream cheese through the foil. "You should have put the bag in the refrigerator," I said. She gnawed. "It would have been simple to put the bag in the refrigerator," I said. "Shut your hole," she said. I shoved her hand. Cream cheese smeared her nostrils. She lay in the bed, slack, still, breathing through her mouth, as if she wouldn't cry and was not crying. I took the bag of groceries and went upstairs. The table was set. She was sweeping the kitchen floor, crying.

The Hand

I SMACKED my little boy. My anger was powerful. Like justice. Then I discovered no feeling in the hand. I said, "Listen, I want to explain the complexities to you." I spoke with seriousness and care, particularly of fathers. He asked, when I finished, if I wanted him to forgive me. I said yes. He said no. Like trumps.

All Right

"I DON'T MIND variations," she said, "but this feels wrong." I said, "It feels all right to me." She said, "To you, wrong is right." I said, "I didn't say right, I said all right." "Big difference," she said. I said, "Yes, I'm critical. My mind never stops. To me almost everything is always wrong. My standard is pleasure. To me, this is all right." She said, "To me it stinks." I said, "What do you like?" She

Phillip

said, "Like I don't like. I'm not interested in being superior to my sensations. I won't live long enough for all right."

Ma

I SAID, "Ma, do you know what happened?" She said, "Oh, my God."

Naked

UGLY OR PLAIN she would have had fewer difficulties cultivating an attractive personality or restricting sex to cortex, but she was so nearly physically perfect as to appear, more than anything, not perfect. Not ugly, not plain, then strikingly not perfect made her also not handsome and not at all sentimentally appealing. In brief, what she was she wasn't, a quality salient in adumbration, unpossessed. She lived a bad metaphor, like the Devil, unable to assimilate paradox to personal life, being no artist and not a religious, suffering spasms of self-loathing in the lonely, moral night. Finally, she smacked a Coke bottle on the rim of the bathtub, mutilated her wrist, then phoned the cops. So clumsy, yet her dinner parties were splendid, prepared at unbelievable speed. She hated to cook. Chewing gum, cigarettes, candy, drugs, alcohol, and taxicabs took her from Monday to Friday. The ambulance attendant—big ironical black man in baggy white trousers—flipped open the medicine cabinet and yelled, "See those barbiturates. You didn't have to make a mess." He dragged her out of the tub by the hair, naked, bleeding. She considered all that impressive, but if I responded to her with a look or tone, she detected my feelings before I did and made them manifest, like a trout slapped out of water by a bear. "You admire my eyes? How about my ass?" I thrilled to her acuity. But exactly then she'd become a stupid girl loosening into sexual mood, and then, then, if I touched her she offered total sprawl, whimpering, "Call me dirty names." I tried to think of her as a homosexual person, not a faggot. She begged me to wear her underpants and walk on my knees. When I demurred, she pissed on the sheets. "You don't love me," she said. "What a waste getting involved with you." Always playing with her flashy, raglike scar, sliding it along the tendons like a watchband.

Better

I PHONED and said, "I feel good, even wonderful. Everything is great. It's been this way for months and it's getting better. Better, better, better. How are you, Ma?" She said, "Me?" I said, "Yes, how are you?" "Me?" she said. "Don't make me laugh."

Getting Lucky

3ρ

LIEBOWITZ MAKES his head out of cigarettes and coffee, goes to the West Side subway,
stands in a screaming iron box, and begins to drift
between shores of small personal misery and fantastic sex, but this morning he felt fingers and, immediately, the flow of his internal life forked into
dialogue between himself—standing man who lived
too much blind from the chest down—and the
other, a soft inquisitive spider pinching the tongue
of his zipper, dragging it toward the iron floor that
boomed in the bones of his rooted feet, boomed in
his legs, and boomed through his unzipped fly.
Thus, with no how-do-you-do, Liebowitz was in the
hand of an invisible stranger. Forty-second Street,
the next stop, was minutes away. Liebowitz tried
to look around. Was everyone groping everyone
else? Fads in Manhattan spread to millions. Liebowitz didn't care to make a fuss, distinguish himself
with a cranky, strictly personal statement. He tried
to be objective, to look around, see what's what in
the IRT. On his left, he saw a Negro woman with a
tired sullen profile and a fat neck the color of liver.

Directly ahead he saw a white man's pale earlobe dangling amid the ravages of a mastoid operation, behind the tension lines of an incipient scowl; his sentiment of being. Against Liebowitz's back were the pillars of indeterminate architecture; palpable and democratic weight. On his right, steeped in a miasma of deodorants and odorants, stood a high-school girl. Thick white makeup, black eyeliner, and lipstick-blotched mouth, which, in the sticky puddle of surrounding skin, seemed to suck and drink her face. Her hair, bleached scraggle, hung. She stared up at an advertisement for suntan lotion, reading and reading and reading, as if it were a letter from God. Telling her perhaps, thought Liebowitz, to wash the crap off her face. Her blotch hung open. She breathed through eight little teeth.

There were others to consider, but Liebowitz decided communications issued from the girl stinking perfume, dreaming of the sun. He didn't look down. He didn't look at her directly. Why not? He was ashamed. Is that any way to feel? It is the way he felt. Besides, Liebowitz thought a direct look might seem aggressive, even threatening, and he didn't want her to stop. Of course, not looking down, he couldn't be sure who was doing it. But whoever it was perhaps couldn't be sure to whom it was being done. Did this make a difference? Yes,

thought Liebowitz. A difference between debauch-
ery and election. Unsought, unanticipated, un-
earned. Not sullied by selfish, inadmissible need.
He didn't think, "Filthy need." He made a bland
face. It felt good. Some might call this "a beautiful
experience."

In effect, 8:30 A.M., going to work, crushed,
breathing poison in a screaming iron box, Liebowitz
was having a beautiful experience. People paid
money for this. He could think of no reason not to
give it a try. Liebowitz was a native New Yorker,
with an invulnerable core of sophistication. He realized suddenly that he felt—beyond pleasure—hip.
After so many years in the subway without feeling,
or feeling he wasn't feeling, he felt. "Getting and
spending," he thought. And now he had gotten
lucky. He believed he had done nothing to account
for it, which was the way it had to be if the experience was miraculous, beautiful, warm, and good.
Like the unaccountable sun shining in the advertisement. Or, for that matter, in the sky. Lucky,
thrilled, beatified. All of it was assumed with silent,
immobilized dignity. He got lucky and floated half
blind, delicious, cool, proud to be a New Yorker. He
floated above a naked ferocity which, he knew, he
couldn't call his own. The emblem and foundation
of his ethical domain—wife, child, responsibility of

feeding them, the "Mr." on his tax forms—and yet, had someone said, "Who belongs to this hard-on?" Liebowitz himself would have led the search. Despite denials and scruples, Liebowitz had a general, friendly hard-on. Even without an object, his sensations were like love.

He came.

Fingers squeezed goodbye, replaced him, zipped up, slipped away. The train stopped at Forty-second Street, doors opened, the crowd dissolved, shuffling huggermugger hugely to the platform. The man with the incipient scowl stepped away. A garden of camellias flashed down his pants leg. Liebowitz looked elsewhere. Bleary, ringing with a chill apocalyptic sense, he was pressed loose and dopey into the crowd's motions. Moving, he began to move himself, popping up on his toes, peering over heads. The girl with the deathly hair had disappeared. On the platform now, amid figures going left, right, and shoving past him toward the train, Liebowitz was seized in a confusion of vectors, but, gathering deep internal force, his direction, himself, he thrust to the right, on his toes, and saw it—limp, ghoulish scraggle flying away like a ghostly light. Exhilaration building, beating in him like hawks, he felt his good luck the second time that morning. To let things end in the dingy, dirty,

booming abyss of the Forty-second Street subway
station would be a desecration of feelings and a
mystery forever, he thought, chasing amid gum
machines, benches, kiosks, trash cans, and innumerable indifferent faces. She went up a flight of
stairs, quickly, quickly, and—painful to Liebowitz
—as if she didn't care to know he was chasing her.
Was there nothing between them? That's what he
wanted to know. He needed psychological consummation. He was a serious human being. He needed
it now and here, in subway light, under low ceil-
ings, in the pressure of heavy moving crowds. He
caught her. Against the door of a ladies' room, the
instant she pressed it, he caught her arm, a thin
bolt, and stopped her flight. "Miss," he said, staring,
beginning to say, "You know me, don't you?" A
weightless, overwrought rag of girl reeked in his
close, tight grip. It whispered, "Get the claw off me,
motherfucker, or I'll kick your balls." Whispering
fire, writhing, murderous. Not a girl. Liebowitz let
go.

The boy twisted into the ladies' room. A dozen
faces bloomed in peripheral vision, like vegetables
of his mind. A lady in a hat said, "Creep." Beneath
the hat, her small shrill eyes recognized Liebowitz.
She said "Creep" as if it were his name. "Mister
Creep," he muttered, pushing away through the

liquid of gathering attention. He didn't run. But he was ready, if anyone moved toward him, to run.

In the brilliant windy street, Liebowitz hailed a cab. Before it stopped, he had the door open. The meter began ticking. Ticking with remorseless, giddy indifference to his personal being and yet, somehow, consonant with himself. Not his heart, not the beat of his viscera, and yet his ticking self, his time, quickly and mercifully growing shorter. "I'll be dead soon," he thought. Tick-tick-tick.

The driver said, *"Where,* mister?"

"Nowhere," said Liebowitz from the creaks and shadows in back.

"You can sit in the park for free. This is costing you."

To Liebowitz, the smug, annoyed superiority of the driver's tone was Manhattan's theme. He ignored it, lit a cigarette, breathed in the consolations of technology, and said, "I want to pay. Shut up."

Storytellers,

Liars, and Bores

I'D WORK AT A STORY until it was imperative to quit and go read it aloud. My friend would listen, then say, "I feel so embarrassed for you." I'd tear up the story. I'd work at a new one until it was imperative to quit and read aloud. My new friend would listen, but wouldn't say good, no good, or not bad. I'd tear up the story.

Meanwhile, I turned to relatives and friends for help. My uncle Zev told me about his years in a concentration camp. "Write it," he said. "You'll make a million bucks." My friend Tony Icona gave me lessons in breaking and entering. Zev's stories I couldn't use. Tony's lessons were good as gold. Criminal life was intermittent and quick. It left me time to work at stories and learn about tearing them up.

One evening, while I was reading to my new friend, she yawned. It was the fifth time I had read this story to her. The hour was late. She had to get up at dawn to leave for work. But I had rewritten the story and had to read it aloud, start to finish. I watched her eyes go fluid, her mouth enlarge. I saw fillings in her teeth and the ciliations of her tongue. By the time she completed her yawn, our friendship had ended.

After I understood so much about stories and friendship, it was easier to write stories and more difficult not to tear them up. There was bad tension between my new friend and me when I tore up a story she liked, but I did it for her sake and mine. Even as she beamed and clapped with delight, I tore it up and stepped on it.

My appeals to Tony Icona for lessons in quick, remunerative work became more frequent. I told him how hard it was to write stories without being a liar or a bore, and there was nothing, nothing, i was unwilling to do for time. He listened, picked his nose, then said if I ended up in the slam doing time, I'd kill myself. He said one person wanted money and power; the other had ideals. Both got money and power. As for himself, he liked walking on the beach in a tight bathing suit and lifting dumbbells in the sun. "That's purity, right?"

When my newest friend said the story was good, but I knew otherwise, I'd be angry and she would begin to cry. She couldn't ignore the solicitous mother in my voice, offering encouragement and music while the story did nothing for itself. She'd let the voice tell her lies, darken her understanding, weaken her will, and incline her toward evil. To make her know it, I broke her nose. Then I couldn't write. "Don't you want to read anything to me?" she'd ask, fingering her nose. "It will never be the same, you know."

When I started again, reading to my newest friend, she'd say, "That reminds me of what happened at work. Can I tell you?" I'd say, "Tell me." She was an astonishing bore. Listening to her, I tore up all my stories, never wrote stories, broke into cars, climbed through windows, and poisoned dogs. She told me what happened to her at work. I made myself ugly, lonely, and miserable.

I explained my condition to Tony Icona, a man to whom I could speak in a theoretical way. He said, "I can't sympathize. You got one leg shorter than the other and you're walking in a circle. But I'll give you a job in my delicatessen. Fifty bucks a week and you keep your tips. If the customers like you, you'll do all right. If they don't, you'll starve and be known as a dope."

The delicatessen, called Horses, was a giant hall with a long bar, mirrors on the walls and ceiling, and a hundred tables. It rang plates and cutlery; twenty chefs boiled at the steam counters and the floor thundered with speeding waiters in black tie, jacket, and shoes. I thundered among them, a napkin slapped across my forearm. At my shoulder a trayload of relishes, bread, and meat. Ladies snatched my elbow and said, "Please, darling. Could you be so wonderful as to bring me a lean pastrami and a piece of cheesecake?" They'd cling and whimper, lips speckled with anticipatory saliva, pleading for complicity in the desire to eat. Then they'd say, "Was it too much to ask, darling? A lean pastrami?" I felt guilty of revolting gristle and the miseries that brought them to Horses. I'd swear there is no such thing as a lean pastrami, pleading for complicity in truth. My tips were small. I was known as a dope. But I studied other waiters and learned to say, "Here, sweetie, just for you—a lean pastrami. Enjoy." My pleasure in their pleasure was their pleasure. My tips were tremendous. When next I learned to say, "Eat, bitch. Stop when you get to the plate," my tips were fantastic.

Sometimes I'd slip into the back of the delicatessen, hide in the meat locker, smoking a cigarette in blood-rancid air, flayed animal tonnage hooked and blazing about my head, and I'd think, "There is no such thing as lean pastrami."

After work I'd see my newest friend, the one who told me boring stories. Her name was Memory. She'd take off my shoes and socks, then wash my feet. A swinish indulgence, but I had the corns of

Odysseus and ancient sentiments. Besides, she had needs in her knees, and it was her way of making me uncritical when she told a story. So much like a lie. Always a bore.

Telling what happened to her at work, she began by saying what time she got up that morning, what the weather was like, and how it differed from the weather report she'd heard the evening before. The last thing she wanted to hear before shutting her eyes was what tomorrow would be like. She had fears of discontinuity. A city girl, nine to five in an office. The days didn't return to her bound each to each by daisies. The weather report was her connection between Monday and Tuesday. One night the man said, "Tomorrow it will not rain." But it rained. Gusty, slapping rain. She said, "Isn't that strange?" She told me what bus she took in the rain, to get the bus that took her near enough to walk, in the rain, to her office. As always, she bought a newspaper to read during coffee break. The newspaper, the coffee break—with Memory I had mortal fears. I hated her story. I wanted her to go on and on. She told me what her boss said before lunch, and what he said after lunch when they chanced to meet in the hallway outside her office as she returned from the ladies' room. She told me that her boss—a married man with three kids—for the first time since she'd been working for him made sexual advances. That was the end of her story. She didn't stop talking or lift her glance to mine. She massaged my corns a bit harder.

I said, "Did you say broom closet?"

"Yes. Isn't that strange?"

Perhaps she'd been telling him a story and he nudged her and glanced significantly at the broom closet, and perhaps he worked her along subtly, as she told the story, sidling her in among brooms, mops, and cans of detergent, as she persisted in her story . . .

"You heard the weather report. You got up in the morning. You noticed the weather, rode a bus, and a married man with three kids made sexual advances in a broom closet."

"The kids weren't there."

I put on my socks.

"You didn't like my story, did you? That's how it is with me. I thrash in a murk of days. But look. Have pity. Take off your socks. I'm skinny and nervous and finicky. I can't tell you stories. I have problems with sublimity. I'm not Kafka."

That night, in a dream, I met Kafka.

A ship had gone down. In one of its rooms, where barnacles were biting the walls, I was reading a story aloud. Sentences issuing from my mouth took the shape of eels and went sliding away among the faces in the room, like elegant metals, slithering in subtleties, which invited and despised attention. When I finished, my uncle Zev rose among the faces, shoving eels aside. He came to me and said nothing about my story, but only that his teeth had been knocked out in the concentration camp. "Write it. Sell it to the movies. Don't be a schmuck. You could entertain people, make a million bucks. They also killed my mother." Tony Icona was there. He said, "Starting next week, you write my menus." With his thumbs he hooked the elastic of his bathing suit and tugged up, molding the genital bulge. The room was full of light, difficult as a headache. It poured through plankton, a glaring diffusion, appropriate to the eyes of a fish. Broken nose appeared, swimming through the palpable light, her mouth a zero. She said, "Have you been introduced to Kafka? He's here, you know." I followed her and was introduced. He shook my hand, then wiped his fingers on his tie.

Kafka an influence .

In the Fifties

IN THE FIFTIES I learned to drive a car. I was frequently in love. I had more friends than now.

When Khrushchev denounced Stalin my roommate shit blood, turned yellow, and lost most of his hair.

I attended the lectures of the excellent E. B. Burgum until Senator McCarthy ended his tenure. I imagined N.Y.U. would burn. Miserable students, drifting in the halls, looked at one another.

In less than a month, working day and night, I wrote a bad novel.

I went to school—N.Y.U., Michigan, Berkeley—much of the time.

I had witty, giddy conversation, four or five nights a week, in a homosexual bar in Ann Arbor.

I read literary reviews the way people suck candy.

Personal relationships were more important to me than anything else.

I had a fight with a powerful fat man who fell on my face and was immovable.

I had personal relationships with football players, jazz musicians, ass-bandits, nympho-maniacs, non-specialized degenerates, and numer-ous Jewish premedical students.

I had personal relationships with thirty-five rhesus monkeys in an experiment on monkey ad-diction to morphine. They knew me as one who shot reeking crap out of cages with a hose.

With four other students I lived in the home of a chiropractor named Leo.

I met a man in Detroit who owned a sub-machine gun; he claimed to have hit Dutch Schultz. I saw a gangster movie that disproved his claim.

I knew two girls who had brains, talent, health, good looks, plenty to eat, and hanged them-selves.

I heard of parties in Ann Arbor where every-one made it with everyone else, including the cat.

I knew card sharks and con men. I liked mar-ginal types because they seemed original and aris-tocratic, living for an ideal or obliged to live it. Ordinary types seemed fundamentally unserious. These distinctions belong to a romantic fop. I didn't think that way too much.

I worked for an evil vanity publisher in Man-hattan.

I worked in a fish-packing plant in Massachu-
setts, on the line with a sincere Jewish poet from
Harvard and three lesbians; one was beautiful, one
grim; both loved the other, who was intelligent. I
loved her too. I dreamed of violating her purity.
They talked among themselves, in creepy whispers,
always about Jung. In a dark corner, away from our
line, old Portuguese men slit fish into open flaps,
flicking out the bones. I could see only their eyes
and knives. I'd arrive early every morning to dash
in and out until the stench became bearable. After
work I'd go to bed and pluck fish scales out of my
skin.

I was a teaching assistant in two English
departments. I graded thousands of freshman
themes. One began like this: "Karl Marx, for that
was his name . . ." Another began like this: "In
Jonathan Swift's famous letter to the Pope . . ." I
wrote edifying comments in the margins. Later I
began to scribble "Awkward" beside everything,
even spelling errors.

I got A's and F's as a graduate student. A professor of English said my attitude wasn't professional. He said that he always read a "good book"
after dinner.

A girl from Indiana said this of me on a

teacher-evaluation form: "It is bad enough to go to an English class at eight in the morning, but to be instructed by a shabby man is horrible."

I made enemies on the East Coast, the West Coast, and in the Middle West. All now dead, sick, or out of luck.

I was arrested, photographed, and finger-printed. In a soundproof room two detectives lectured me on the American way of life, and I was charged with the crime of nothing. A New York cop told me that detectives were called "defectives."

I had an automobile accident. I did the mambo. I had urethritis and mononucleosis.

In Ann Arbor, a few years before the advent of Malcolm X, a lot of my friends were black. After Malcolm X, almost all my friends were white. They admired John F. Kennedy.

In the fifties I smoked marijuana, hash, and opium. Once I drank absinthe. Once I swallowed twenty glycerine caps of peyote. The social effects of "drugs," unless sexual, always seemed tedious. But I liked people who inclined the drug way. Especially if they didn't proselytize. I listened to long conversations about the phenomenological weirdness of familiar reality and the great spiritual questions this entailed—for example, "Do you think Wallace Stevens is a head?"

In the Fifties

I witnessed an abortion.

I was godless, but I thought the fashion of intellectual religiosity more despicable. I wished that I could live in a culture rather than study life among the cultured.

I drove a Chevy Bel Air eighty-five miles per hour on a two-lane blacktop. It was nighttime. Intermittent thick white fog made the headlights feeble and diffuse. Four others in the car sat with the strict silent rectitude of catatonics. If one of them didn't admit to being frightened, we were dead. A Cadillac, doing a hundred miles per hour, passed us and was obliterated in the fog. I slowed down.

I drank Old Fashioneds in the apartment of my friend Julian. We talked about Worringer and Spengler. We gossiped about friends. Then we left to meet our dates. There was more drinking. We all climbed trees, crawled in the street, and went to a church. Julian walked into an elm, smashed his glasses, vomited on a lawn, and returned home to memorize Anglo-Saxon grammatical forms. I ended on my knees, vomiting into a toilet bowl, repeatedly flushing the water to hide my noises. Later I phoned New York so that I could listen to the voices of my parents, their Yiddish, their English, their logics.

I knew a professor of English who wrote impassioned sonnets in honor of Henry Ford.

I played freshman varsity basketball at N.Y.U. and received a dollar an hour for practice sessions and double that for games. It was called "meal money." I played badly, too psychological, too worried about not studying, too short. If pushed or elbowed during a practice game, I was ready to kill. The coach liked my attitude. In his day, he said, practice ended when there was blood on the boards. I ran back and forth, in urgent sneakers, through my freshman year. Near the end I came down with pleurisy, quit basketball, started smoking more.

I took classes in comparative anatomy and chemistry. I took classes in Old English, Middle English, and modern literature. I took classes and classes.

I fired a twelve-gauge shotgun down the hallway of a railroad flat into a couch pillow.

My roommate bought the shotgun because of his gambling debts. He expected murderous thugs to come for him. I'd wake in the middle of the night listening for a knock, a cough, a footstep, wondering how to identify myself as not him when they broke through our door.

My roommate was an expensively dressed kid from a Chicago suburb. Though very intelligent, he suffered in school. He suffered with girls though he was handsome and witty. He suffered with boys though he was heterosexual. He slept on three mattresses and used a sun lamp all winter. He bathed, oiled, and perfumed his body daily. He wanted soft, sweet joys in every part, but when some whore asked if he'd like to be beaten with a garrison belt he said yes. He suffered with food, eating from morning to night, loading his pockets with fried pumpkin seeds when he left for class, smearing caviar paste on his filet mignons, eating himself into a monumental face of eating because he was eating. Then he killed himself.

A lot of young, gifted people I knew in the fifties killed themselves. Only a few of them continue walking around.

I wrote literary essays in the turgid, tumescent manner of darkest Blackmur.

I used to think that someday I would write a fictional version of my stupid life in the fifties.

I was a waiter in a Catskill hotel. The captain of the waiters ordered us to dance with the female guests who appeared in the casino without escorts and, as much as possible, fuck them. A professional *tummler* walked the grounds. Wherever he saw a group of people merely chatting, he thrust in quickly and created a tumult.

I heard the Budapest String Quartet, Dylan Thomas, Lester Young and Billie Holiday together, and I saw Pearl Primus dance, in a Village night-club, in a space two yards square, accompanied by an African drummer about seventy years old. His hands moved in spasms of mathematical complexity at invisible speed. People left their tables to press close to Primus and see the expression in her face, the sweat, the muscles, the way her naked feet seized and released the floor.

Eventually I had friends in New York, Ann Arbor, Chicago, Berkeley, and Los Angeles.

I did the cha-cha, wearing a tux, at a New Year's party in Hollywood, and sat at a table with Steve McQueen. He'd become famous in a TV series about a cowboy with a rifle. He said he didn't know which he liked best, acting or driving a racing car. I thought he was a silly person and then realized he thought I was. I met a few other famous people who said something. One night, in a yellow Porsche, I circled Manhattan with Jack Kerouac. He recited passages, perfectly remembered from his book reviews, to the sky. His manner was ironical, sweet, and depressing.

I had a friend named Chicky who drove his chopped, blocked, stripped, dual-exhaust Ford convertible, while vomiting out the fly window, into a telephone pole. He survived, lit a match to see if the engine was all right, and it blew up in his face. I saw him in the hospital. Through his bandages he said that ever since high school he'd been trying to kill himself. Because his girlfriend wasn't good-looking enough. He was crying and laughing while he pleaded with me to believe that he really had been trying to kill himself because his girlfriend wasn't good-looking enough. I told him that I was going out with a certain girl and he told me that he had fucked her once but it didn't matter because I could take her away and live somewhere else. He was a Sicilian kid with a face like Caravaggio's angels of debauch. He'd been educated by priests and nuns. When his hair grew back and his face healed, his mind healed. He broke up with his girl-friend. He wasn't nearly as narcissistic as other men I knew in the fifties.

I knew one who, before picking up his dates, ironed his dollar bills and powdered his testicles. And another who referred to women as "cockless wonders" and used only their family names—for example, "I'm going to meet Goldberg, the cockless wonder." Many women thought he was extremely attractive and became his sexual slaves. Men didn't like him.

I had a friend who was dragged down a courthouse stairway, in San Francisco, by her hair. She'd wanted to attend the House Un-American hearings. The next morning I crossed the Bay Bridge to join my first protest demonstration. I felt frightened and embarrassed. I was bitter about what had happened to her and the others she'd been with. I expected to see thirty or forty people like me, carrying hysterical placards around the courthouse until the cops bludgeoned us into the pavement. About two thousand people were there. I marched beside a little kid who had a bag of marbles to throw under the hoofs of the horse cops. His mother kept saying, "Not yet, not yet." We marched all day. That was the end of the fifties.

Reflections of a Wild Kid

M ANDELL ASKED if she had ever been celebrated.

"Celebrated?"

"I mean your body, has your body ever been celebrated?" Then, as if to refine the question: "I mean, like, has your body, like, been celebrated?"

"My body has never been celebrated."

She laughed politely. A laugh qualified by her sense of Liebowitz in the bedroom. She was polite to both of them and good to neither. Certainly not to Liebowitz, who, after all, wanted Mandell out of the apartment. Did she care what he wanted? He was her past, a whimsical recrudescence, trapped in her bedroom. He'd waited in there for an hour. He could wait another hour. As far as she knew, he had cigarettes. But, in that hour, as he smoked his cigarettes, his bladder had begun to feel like a cantaloupe. He strained to lift the window. The more he strained, the more he felt his cantaloupe.

"I mean really celebrated," said Mandell, as if she'd answered nothing.

Perhaps, somehow, she urged Mandell to go

on. Perhaps she wanted Liebowitz to hear Mandell's witty questions, his lovemaking. Liebowitz didn't care what she wanted. His last cigarette had been smoked. He wanted to piss. He drew the point of a nail file down the sides of the window, trailing a thin peel, a tiny scream in the paint. Again he strained to lift the window. It wouldn't budge. At that moment he noticed wall-to-wall carpeting. Why did he notice? Because he couldn't piss on it. "Amazing," he thought, "how we perceive the world. Stand on a mountain and you think it's remarkable that you can't jump off."

"My body," said Mandell, "has been celebrated."

Had that been his object all along? Liebowitz wondered why Mandell hadn't been more direct, ripping off his shirt, flashing nipples in her face: "Let's celebrate." She was going to marry a feeb. But that wasn't Liebowitz's business. He had to piss. He had no other business.

"I mean, you know, like my body, like, has been celebrated," said Mandell, again refining his idea. Despite his pain, it was impossible for Liebowitz not to listen—the sniveling syntax, the whining diction—he tasted every phrase. In that hour, as increasingly he had to piss, he came to know Mandell, through the wall, palpably to know him. Some smell, some look, even something about the way he combed his hair, reached Liebowitz through the wall. Bad blood, thought Liebowitz.

He remembered Nietzsche's autobiographical remark: "I once sensed the proximity of a herd of cows . . . merely because milder and more philanthropic thoughts came back to me." How true. Thoughts can be affected by invisible animals. Liebowitz had never even seen Mandell. As for Joyce, a shoe lying on its side, in the middle of her carpet—scuffed, bent, softened by the stride of her uncelebrated body—suffused the bedroom with her presence, the walking foot, strong well-shaped ankle, peasant hips rocking with motive power, elegant neck, fleshy boneless Semitic face. A warm receptive face until she spoke. Then she had personality. That made her seem taller, slightly forbidding, even robust. She was robust—heavy bones, big head, dense yellow-brown hair—and her voice, a flying bird of personality. Years had passed. Seeing the hair again and Joyce still fallow beneath it saddened Liebowitz. But here was Mandell. She had time.

"Has it been five years?" asked Liebowitz, figuring seven. "You sound wonderful, Joyce." She said he sounded "good." He regretted "wonderful," but noticed no other reserve in her voice, and just as he remembered, she seemed still to love the telephone, coming at him right through the machine, much the thing, no later than this minute. When his other phone rang he didn't reach for it, thus letting her hear and understand how complete was his attention. She understood. She went on directly about some restaurant, insisting let's eat there. He didn't even consider not. She'd said, almost immediately, she was getting married to Mandell, a professor.

Did Liebowitz feel jealousy? He didn't ask professor of what or where does he teach. Perhaps he felt jealousy; but, listening to her and nodding compliments at the wall, he listened less to what she said than to how she spoke in echoes. Not of former times, but approximately these things, in approximately the same way, he felt, had been said in grand rooms, by wonderful people. Joyce brought him the authority of echoes. And she delivered herself, too, a hundred thirty-five pounds of shank and dazzle, even in her questions: "Have you seen . . . ?" "Have you heard . . . ?" About plays, movies, restaurants, Jacqueline Kennedy. Nothing about his wife, child, job. Was she indifferent? embarrassed? hostile? In any case, he liked her impetuosity; she poked, checked his senses. He liked her. Joyce Wolf, on the telephone. He remembered that cabbies and waiters liked her. She could make fast personal jokes with policemen and bellhops. She tipped big. A hundred nobodies knew her name, her style. Always *en passant,* very much here and not here at all. He liked her tremendously, he felt revived. Not reliving a memory, but right now, on the telephone, living again a moment of his former life. For the first time, as it were, that he didn't have to live it. She has magic, he thought; art. Merely in her voice, she was an event. She called him back, through time, to herself. Despite his grip on the phone, knees under the desk, feet on the floor, he felt like a man slipping from a height, deliciously. He said he would meet her uptown in forty minutes. Did he once live this way? Liebowitz shook his head; smirked. He was a wild kid once.

On his desk lay a manuscript that had to be edited, and a contract he had to work on. There was also an appointment with an author . . . but, in the toilet with electric razor and toothbrush, Liebowitz purged his face of the working day and, shortly thereafter, walked into a chic Hungarian restaurant on the Upper East Side. She arrived twenty minutes later; late; but in a black sleeveless dress. Very smart. It gave her a look that seized the day, the feeling and idea of it. She hadn't just come

to meet him; she described their moment and
meaning, in a garment. She appeared. Late; but
who, granted such knowledge, could complain?
Liebowitz felt flattered and grateful. He took her
hands. She squeezed his hands. He kissed her
cheek. "Joyce." The hair, white smile, hips—he
remembered, he looked, looked. "It was good of you
to call me." He looked at her. He looked into his
head. She was there, too, this minute's Joyce Wolf
who once got them to the front of lines, to seats
when the show was sold out, to tables, tables near
windows, to parties. Sold out, you say? At the box
office, in her name, two tickets were waiting. Then
Liebowitz remembered, once, for a ballet, she had
failed to do better than standing room. He hadn't
wanted to go. He certainly hadn't wanted to stand.
Neither had she. But tickets had been sold out to
this ballet. Thousands wanted to go. Liebowitz remembered how she began making phone calls,
scratching at the numbers till her fingernail tore.
That evening, pelvises pressed to a velvet rope, they
stood amid hundreds of ballet lovers jammed into a
narrow aisle. The effluvia of alimentary canals
hung about their heads. Blindfolded, required to
guess, Liebowitz would have said they were in a
delicatessen. Lights dimmed. There was a thrilling
hush. Joyce whispered, "How in God's name can

anyone live outside New York?" She nudged him and pointed at a figure seated in the audience. Liebowitz looked, thrusting his head forward to show appreciation of her excitement, her talent for recognizing anyone in New York in almost total darkness. "See! See!" Liebowitz nodded greedily. His soul poured toward a glint of skull floating amid a thousand skulls. He begged, "Who? Who is it?" He wasn't sure that he looked at the correct glint of skull, yet he felt on the verge of extraordinary illumination. Then a voice wailed into his back, "I can't see." Liebowitz twisted about, glanced down. A short lady, staring up at him, pleaded with her whole face. "I can't see." He twisted forward and said, "Move a little, Joyce. Let her up against the rope." Joyce whispered, "This is the jungle, schmuck. Tell her to grow another head." He was impressed. During the ballet he stood with the velvet rope in his fists, the woman's face between his shoulder blades, and now, as he went uptown in the cab, his mouth was so dry he couldn't smoke. After all these years, still impressed. Joyce got them tickets. She knew. She got. Him, for example—virtually a bum in those days, but nice-looking, moody, a complement to her, he supposed. Perhaps a girl with so much needed someone like him—a misery. Not that she was without misery. She

this. Joyce is a tough predatory city woman

worked as private secretary to an investment broker, a shrewd, ugly Russian with a hunchback and a limp. "Hey, collich girl, make me a phone call." After work she used to meet Liebowitz, hunching, dragging a foot, and she would shout, "Hey, collich. Hey, collich girl, kiss my ass." They'd laugh with relief and malice; but sometimes she met Liebowitz in tears. Once the Russian even hit her. "In a Longchamps, during lunch hour," she said. "He knocked me on the floor in front of all those people eating lunch." Liebowitz remembered her screaming at him: "Even if there had been a reason." He stopped trying to justify the horror. It got to him. "Gratuitous sadism!" Liebowitz raged. He'd go next morning and punch the Russian in the mouth. The next morning, in Italian sunglasses, Joyce left for the office. Alone. Five foot seven, she walked seven foot five, a Jewish girl passing for Jewish in tough financial circles. Liebowitz smoked a cigarette, punched his hand. Liebowitz remembered:

The sunglasses—tough, tragic, fantastically clever—looked terrific. She knew what to wear, precisely the item that said it. Those sunglasses were twenty punches in the mouth. She'd wear them all day, even at the typewriter. The Russian would feel, between himself and the college girl, an immensity. He'd know what he was, compared to her in those black, estranging glasses. Liebowitz felt an intellectual pang; his reflections had gone schmuckway. Beginning again:

Joyce made two hundred and fifty dollars a week. With insults and slaps, the Russian gave tips on the market. The year she lived with Liebowitz, Joyce made over a hundred thousand dollars. Liebowitz, then a salesman in a shoe store, made eighty dollars a week hunkering over corns. He had rotten moods, no tips on anything; he had a lapsed candidacy for the Ph.D. in philosophy and a girl with access to the pleasures of Manhattan. Her chief pleasure—moody Liebowitz. In truth, he never hated the Russian. He pitied Joyce; for a hundred thousand dollars she ate shit. The sunglasses symbolized shame. Liebowitz remembered:

Twenty-four years old, a virgin when she met Liebowitz, who took her on their first date. "I don't know how it happened," she said. "Two minutes ago I had some idea of myself." Liebowitz replied, "Normal." She'd been surprised, overwhelmed by his intensity. She'd never met a man so hungry. Now he was cool, like a hoodlum. "Where's your shower?" He wondered if he hadn't been worse to her than the Russian. Hidden in the bedroom, crouched in pain, Liebowitz made big eyes and held out his hands, palms up, like a man begging for apples. He'd had certain needs. She'd been good to him—the tickets, the parties, and calling now to announce her forthcoming marriage; invite him to dinner. It was touching. Liebowitz had to piss. He remembered that, walking into the restaurant, he'd had an erection. Perhaps that explained the past; also the present, running to meet her as if today were yesterday. Then they strolled in the park. Then they went to her apartment for a drink. Life is mystery, thought Liebowitz. He wondered if he dared, after all these years, after she'd just told him she was getting married, put his hand on her knee; her thigh; under the black dress where time, surrendering to truth, ceased to be itself. The doorbell.

"Don't answer," said Liebowitz.

"Maybe it's someone else," she said, her voice as frightened as his.

It wasn't somebody else. Liebowitz opted for the bedroom. Then he was tearing at the window, wild to piss.

"Didn't you say you were going to work this evening?"

"Did I say that?"

Mandell had had a whimsy impulse. Here he was, body freak, father of Joyce's unborn children. She could have done better, thought Liebowitz.

Consider himself, Liebowitz. But seven years had passed since he'd put his hand on her thigh. A woman begins to feel desperate. Still—Joyce Wolf, her style, her hips—she could have done better than Mandell, thought Liebowitz, despite her conviction—her boast—that Mandell wasn't just any professor of rhetoric and communication art. "He loves teaching—speech, creative writing, anything —and every summer at Fire Island he writes a novel of ideas. None are published yet, but he doesn't care about publication. People say his novels are very good. I couldn't say, but he talks about his writing all the time. He really cares."

Liebowitz could see Mandell curled over his typewriter. Forehead presses the keys. Sweat fills his bathing-suit jock. It's summertime on Fire Island. Mandell is having an idea to stick in one of his novels. "You know, of course, my firm only does textbooks." Joyce said she knew, yet looked surprised, changed the subject. Liebowitz felt ashamed. Of course she knew. Why had he been crude? Did he suppose that she hadn't really wanted to telephone him, that she was using him as a source of tickets? What difference? He had an erection, a purpose; she had Mandell, novelist of ideas, celebrated for his body. "He is terribly jealous of you," she said. "It was long ago, I was a kid, and he wasn't even in the picture. But he's jealous. He's the kind who wonders about a girl's former lovers. Not that he's weird or anything, just social. He's terrific in bed. I'll bet you two could be friends."

"Does he know I'm seeing you tonight?" Liebowitz's hand had ached for her knee. Her voice had begun to cause brain damage and had to be stopped. It was getting late, there was nothing more to say. She laughed again. Marvelous sound, thought Liebowitz, almost like laughter. He was nearly convinced now that she deserved Mandell. But why didn't she send him away or suggest they go out? Was it because Liebowitz's firm didn't do novels? Was he supposed to listen? burn with jealousy? He burned to piss.

"Is something wrong, Joycie?"

Mandell didn't understand. Did she seem slightly cool, too polite? Did she laugh too much?

"I wanted to talk to you about my writing, but really, Joycie, is something, like, wrong?"

"What do you mean? There's nothing wrong. I just thought you'd be working tonight."

Mandell was embarrassed, a little hurt, unable to leave. Of course. How could he leave with her behaving that polite way? Mandell was just as trapped as Liebowitz, who, bent and drooling, gaped at a shoe, a dressing table, combs, brushes, cosmetics, a roll of insulation tape . . . and, before he knew what he had in mind, Liebowitz seized the tape. He laid two strips, in an X, across a windowpane, punched the nail file into the heart of the X, and gently pulled away the tape with sections of broken glass. Like Robinson Crusoe. Trapped, isolated—yet he could make himself comfortable. Liebowitz felt proud. Mainly, he felt searing release. Liebowitz pissed.

Through the hole in the windowpane, across an echoing air shaft, a long shining line—burning, arcing, resonant—as he listened to Mandell. "I have a friend who says my novels are *like* writing, but not real writing, you get it?" Liebowitz shook his head, thinking, "Some friend," as he splashed brick wall and a window on the other side of the air shaft, and though he heard yelling, heard nothing relevant to Robinson Crusoe, and though he saw a man's face, continued pissing on that face, yelling from the window, on the other side of the air shaft.

"A good neighborhood," thought Liebowitz. "The police won't take long." He wondered what to say, how to say it, and zipped up hurriedly. In the dressing-table mirror he saw another face, his own, bloated by pressure, trying not to cry. "According to that face," he thought, "a life is at stake." His life was at stake and he couldn't grab a cab. Mandell was still there, whining about his writing. Joyce couldn't interrupt and say go home. Writers are touchy. He might get mad and call off the marriage. Liebowitz had no choice but to prepare a statement. "My name, officers, is Liebowitz." Thus he planned to begin. Not brilliant. Appropriate. He'd chuckle in a jolly, personable way. A regular fellow, not a drunk or a maniac. Mandell was shrill and peevish: "Look here, look here. My name is Mandell. I'm a professor of rhetoric and communication art at a college. And a novelist. This is ironic, but it is only a matter of circumstances and I have no idea what it means."

A strange voice said, "Don't worry, Professor, we'll explain later."

Joyce said, "This is a silly mistake. I'm sure you chaps have a lot to do—"

Mandell cut in: "Take your hands off me. And you shut up, Joyce. I've had enough of this crap. Like, show me the lousy warrant or, like, get the hell out. No Nazi cops push me around. Joyce, call someone. I'm not without friends. Call someone."

The strange voice said, "Hold the creep."

With hatred Mandell was screaming, "No, no, don't come with me. I don't want you to come with me, you stupid bitch. Call someone. Get help." The hall door shut. The bedroom door opened. Joyce

[84]

was staring at Liebowitz. "You hear what happened? How can you sit there and stare at me? I've never felt this way in my life. Look at you. Lepers could be screwing at your feet. Do you realize what happened?"

Liebowitz shrugged yes mixed a little with no.

"I see," she said. "I see. You're furious because you had to sit in here. What could I do? What could I say? You're furious as hell, aren't you?"

Liebowitz didn't answer. He felt a bitter strength in his position. Joyce began pinching her thighs to express suffering. Unable to deal with herself across the room from him, she came closer to where he sat on the bed. Liebowitz said, "The cops took the putz away." His tone revealed no anger and let her sit down beside him. "It's horrible. It's humiliating," she said. "They think he pissed out the window. He called me a stupid bitch." Liebowitz said, "You might be a stupid bitch, but you look as good to me now as years ago. In some ways, better." His hand was on her knee. It seemed to him a big hand, full of genius and power. He felt proud to consider how these qualities converged in himself. Joyce's mouth and eyes grew slow, as if the girl behind them had stopped jumping. She glanced at his hand. "I must make a phone call," she said softly, a little urgently, and started to

rise. Liebowitz pressed down. She sat. "It wouldn't
be right," she said, and then, imploringly, "Would
you like to smoke a joint?"

"No."

She has middle-class habits, he thought.

"It wouldn't be right," she said, as if to remind
him of something, not to insist on it. But what's
right, what's wrong to a genius? Liebowitz, forty
years old, screwed her like a nineteen-year-old
genius.

This
P. is not
admirable
certainly; not
even likable.
I'm hardpressed
to find redeeming
features.

Downers

Beyond Orgasm

SHE DIDN'T LIKE ME. So I phoned her every day. I announced the new movies, concerts, art exhibits. I talked them up, excitements out there, claiming them in my voice. Not to like me was not to like the world. Then I asked her out. Impossible to say no. I appeared at her door in a witty hat, a crazy tie. Sometimes I changed my hair style. I was various, talking, dancing, waving my arms. I was the world. But she didn't like me. If she weren't so sweet, if she had will power, if she didn't miss the other guy so much, she'd have said, "Beat it, you're irrelevant." But she was in pain, confused about herself. The other guy had dumped her. I owed him a debt. It took the form of hatred, although, if not for him, she wouldn't have needed me. Not that she did. She needed my effort, not me. Me, she didn't like. Discouraged, sad, thinking I'd overdone this bad act and maybe I didn't like her all that much, I said, "Let's go to the restaurant next door, have dinner, say goodbye." She seemed reluctant, even frightened. I wondered if, in such decisive gestures,

there was hope. She said, "Not there." I wondered
if it was his hangout, or a restaurant she used to
enjoy with him. I insisted. "Please," she said, "any
other restaurant." But I needed this concession.
She'd never given me anything else. For two men
I'd talked and danced, even in bed. I insisted.
Adamant. Shaking. "Only that restaurant." She
took my arm. We walked briskly in appreciation of
my feelings. As we entered the restaurant, she
pulled back. I recognized him—alone, sitting at a
table. Him. The other guy. My soul flew into the
shape of his face. He yawned. Nothing justifies
hate like animal simplicity. "Look. He's yawning.
What a swine." Was it a show of casual vulnerability? Contempt? She pulled my arm. I didn't budge.
I stared. His eyes squeezed to dashes. I heard the
mock whimper of yawns. He began scratching the
tablecloth. Two waiters ran to his side with questions of concern. His yawn was half his face. Bat-
like whimpers issued from it. Jawbones had
locked, fiercely, absolutely. He needed help. My fist
was ready. She cried, begging, dragging me away. I
let her. That night was our beginning. Whenever I
yawned at her, she'd laugh and plead, "Stop it." Her
admiration of me extended to orgasm. Even beyond. It was not unmixed with fear.

The Pinch

NIGHT CAME. I went to the window. My mother said, "What are you looking at?" I looked. She stood beside me and touched my arm. "What are you looking at?" Swinging through the windy blackness were spooky whites. My mother looked. She said, "Sheets. Sheets on a line." I saw pale neurasthenics licking bodies of the air. She said, "You don't believe me? Put on your coat." She took me to the alley and held my hand. We stood beneath the sheets. I heard a dull spasmodic flap as the wind released them. We went home. I stood at the window. "Sheets on a line," she said. I was crying. She pinched my arm. "I pinched your arm," she said. Her face came closer to mine, as if to bring my face closer to mine, pleading, "I will pinch your arm."

Lefty-Righty

RUNNING IN A FAST GAME, I was pushed and went running off the court into a brick wall. My palm flattened against brick, driving shock into my wrist. The city wasn't big enough for that pain. Other players left the game to watch me. Buildings grumbled in their roots. In tiny grains of concrete I saw recriminations. I rolled onto my back. A circle of faces looked down. I looked at the sky and didn't scream. I might have broken my nose, my cheek, my left wrist. Why had it been the right? Then someone replaced me in the game. It resumed before I left the playground. I was abolished by tenements. For six weeks I wore a plaster cast. It itched in warm rooms. The left hand held forks and spoons, combed my hair, buttoned shirts. It could soon knot a tie. But it took passes like a wooden claw. It threw them like a catapult, not a hand. Broken this way, a wild animal would have been noticed, killed, got out of sight. I appeared daily, lingering on the sidelines, shuffling in among the healthy when they formed teams. Not saying a word, I begged: "Choose me." Nobody looked in my direction, but being there gave me a right. Begrudged, but a right. Sooner or later, at least once a day, I'd be chosen. Any team I played on lost. Before and after games, alone, I practiced running to my left, dribbling lefty, shooting lefty. I became less bad. The left hand became a hand. In a tough, fast game, a few days after the cast was removed, my opponent said, "Hey, man, you a lefty or a righty?" I mumbled, "Lefty-righty." My team won easily. He came up to me and whispered, "How do you wipe your ass?" Out of noblesse oblige, I laughed. He grinned like a grateful ape, then offered me a cigarette, which I declined.

Angry

I HEARD that he had come to town. He hadn't called me. I supposed he was angry. I became angry, too. I wouldn't call him. When he called I was polite and agreed to go to his place. Dinner was pleasant. We talked for hours. When I yawned he raised new subjects, offered more cognac. His wife offered more to eat. I lighted another cigarette. His child, a two-year-old boy, came into the room. It seemed appropriate, delightful. But something was wrong with him. A distortion, quite serious, impossible not to notice. He was told to say hello, then sent back to bed. The air resisted words. We became flat and opaque. I put out my cigarette. They didn't try to detain me. We shook hands at the door.

What You Haven't Done

WILDLY PILED, pinned black hair. A face of busyness interrupted.

"Ever think of anyone but yourself?"

"You."

"Bullshit."

I shut the door, waited. Nothing changed. Bullshit banged my head.

"I haven't cleaned my apartment or done my shopping. My cat has to go to the vet. My mother will phone in twenty minutes."

I rushed forward, hugged her, kissed her neck —deep—as if to plug a hole. She hung in my arms. I quit kissing. She looked at me with fatigue, an expression like apology but distinct from it. Then she touched my hand.

"Take off your clothes," I said.

"So much to do."

"Everything off."

Her face flashed through spaces in her black wool sweater. Her skirt dropped. She walked away naked, rapid, matter-of-fact, and sat on the bed.

"I want to know something," I said. "What have you never done with another man?" I sat beside her.

"This," she groaned, then plucked out hairpins.

"A man used to ask a woman if she's a virgin. Now I ask you a question of the heart."

"What do you want to know, exactly?"

"What you haven't done . . ."

She smacked her fists to her ears. "Cleaned my apartment. Expect a phone call. Cat has to go to the vet."

The Broken Leg

MY AUNT tapped the spot and described the pain. Big Doctor sneered, "Nothing is wrong with your knee." She tapped again. Described the pain. Big Doctor slapped his own knee and said, "Nothing is wrong." She said, "Just give me a prescription." He refused to prescribe even an aspirin. My aunt said, "My knee is sick. My knee is in pain. That pleases you." He glanced at his calendar, set a date for the knife. My aunt went home. She read books on diet and health and started doing yoga exercises. Her knee felt better. There was no pain. She dressed and hurried out to see Big Doctor—blue-tinted hair, maroon lipstick, necklace, bracelets, rings, girdle, stockings, high heels—running down Broadway, singing, "Big Doctor, my knee is better," running, running . . .

Pornographic

THE GIRL had Oriental eyes with blue pupils in a round, white Oriental face. Blue pupils beneath epicanthic folds in the innocent emptiness of a round face. Her mouth was heavy and long and linear. Beautifully curled. The camera identified it with the genitals of her colleagues, perhaps a dozen males bearing temperamentally stiff or floppy pricks. Opposed to her mouth, not beautiful; but problematic or hysterical. Relieved of this or that prick, her mouth smiled. Personal light went un-pricked, smiling along abdominal walls to their owners, reassuring them: "We are actors in a pornographic movie. Nothing is at stake." Then it recurred quickly to cinematic obligations—to suck and lick with conviction. The camera adhered to it, lucid, neutral, ubiquitous. The camera's look. Nearly like her mouth, assimilating advertise-ments of the male, but only in its totalitarian look-ing. The camera's invincible distance. The look of looking.

Being Moral

"I'VE GOT A PROBLEM," she said. "I'm ob-sessed by trivial reflections. When I brush my teeth, I think people are starving. Yet I'm determined to brush my teeth because it's moral. But brushing makes me hungry. Eat, brush, eat, brush. I'm afraid someone will have to put a bullet in my head to save me from myself. Being moral is a luxury, isn't it? No, it's asking the question. That's why I spend my time stealing, fucking, and taking dope."

Listening

EVERY SEAT was taken. Students sat on the floor and window ledges. They barely moved. Nobody smoked. He took off his raincoat, laid it on the desk. At the end of the hour he'd look for his hat. Which was on his head. He arrived with a handkerchief pressed to his lips, wiping away his breakfast. Zipping his fly. He ground fingers into his ears, as if digging for insects. Then, putting his hands in his trouser pockets, he tumbled his prunes. We watched. His loneliness made revelations. Dirty fingernails, nicotine stains, one shoelace a clot of knots. Students followed him to his office. Papers on his desk, piled level with his chest, smelled of rotting food. They defeated conversation. He'd invite you to sit. The chair looked greasy. The floor was splotched with coffee, dried oils, trapped grit. No walls, only book pressure, with small gaps in the volumes for shaving equipment, mirror, hairbrush, and toothbrush. "Please sit." They never stayed long. They rushed to his classes. Girls with long hair, shampooed five times a week, gave him feeling looks, accumulating knees and ankles in the front row. His life in a pool of eye-balls. He didn't know he was there. He'd begin. The silence was awesome, as if subsequent to a boom. Nobody had been talking, yet a space cleared, a hole blown out of nothing for his voice. It was like a blues piano rumbling in the abyss; meditations in pursuit of meditations. His course, "Philosophy 999: Great Issues," was also called "Introduction to Thought" and "History of Consciousness." He taught one course. He'd blow his nose. The hand-kerchief still in his hand, he too observed a silence. Listening. To listen was to think. We listened to him listening. World gathered into mind. Some-times the hour ended that way, in silence, then spontaneous applause. His authenticity was in-superable. He scratched his buttocks, looked out the window. Once he said, "Winter." A girl cried, "Janu-ary," eager for dialogue. Toward the end, he sat in a chair, elbows on knees, and shut one eye. Through the other, with heavy head cocked, he squinted at the ceiling, as if a last point were up there. After taking his course, students couldn't speak without shutting one eye, addressing the ceiling. At a party I saw a girl shut one eye and scratch her buttocks. That was in Chicago, years later, after he was dead. I went up to her, shut one eye, and asked, "Can you tell me one thing, any particular thing he said? He never published a book, not even a book review." She looked at me as if at moral scum.

The Conversation

WE TWISTED up together in New York. Intimacy was insult; love could hate. Then I went away. Years passed. He came to visit. It wasn't easy to talk. Finally I mentioned a pornographic movie. He said, "Which pornographic movie?" I said, "You distinguish carefully among them?" He didn't smile. As if to spare my feelings, he began talking about New York. The complexities, the intensities. I listened with humble attention, trying to remember the title of the pornographic movie. Naked bodies came to mind, agitating to the impulses of community. If I'd remembered the title, I'd have screamed it. But I couldn't remember. He went on, the Metropolis of Total Excitement flying out of his mouth. Later, I asked him to see the other rooms in my house. It was a corny gesture. But he stood right up and made an urbane shrug, suggesting revulsion or eagerness. I led him out of the foyer. When we came to my study I pushed the windows wide. "Trees, birds," I said. He grinned a mellow hook and didn't glance at the view. He said, "Do you know about Sartre's study?" I said, "No; so what." He said, "Jean-Paul Sartre's study gives out upon great Parisian avenues. They converge in his desk. Endless human traffic converges in Jean-Paul Sartre's desk." I said, "Actually, I hate trees and birds. They make me sick." He giggled, poked my arm, told me to go fuck myself. "Why?" I asked. He said, "Because you're deficient in social hormones." I laughed, "That's the title of the pornographic movie. *Social Hormones.*" I laughed, but his remark felt incisive; I couldn't be sure what he meant. In the foyer again, I shook his hand, slapped his back. He was rattling goodbyes, edging out the door, looking at me with exhilaration.

The Snake

THE ROAD, crowded by woods on either side, turned whimsically as a line of smoke, taking its own peculiar way, unpredictable, inevitable as fate, but I continued driving hard, pressing it until I'd go too fast and have to slow suddenly, holding the turn until I could press again, fast, faster. It was like that for hours. Me against it. I was tired. She was bored, nervous, giddy. Whenever I said anything, she'd say, "Awfully Jewish of you." She giggled, tried to read a magazine, brushed her hair. I smoked cigarettes, attacked the road, and stopped talking to her. She played with the radio knobs, pulled up her skirt, stroked her legs. Then I noticed a brown snake. I stopped the car. "Drive over it," she said. "Don't you leave this car." I left the car. She moaned, "Please." The snake was thicker than my foot. Blinkless eyes; medals of mud against its sides; tiny sticks of grass embedded in the mud. Ants crawled across the scales. She said, "Please." Her voice was bright, meaningless, far away. I crouched and reached slowly—toward the neck—a necessity. It would fill my fist; whip; hiss. She yelled, "My mother was bitten by a brown snake like that, you New York asshole." I grabbed it. I screamed. She tumbled out of the car. I lifted the snake. It hung. It was a dead snake. We got back into the car and sat there quietly. Then I asked her to marry me. She said, "O.K." We laughed and fucked until dark.

Liver

"EVERYTHING IS FINE," I said. My mother said, "I hope so." I said, "It is, it is." My mother said, "I hope so." I said, "Everything is wonderful. Couldn't be better. How do you feel?" My mother said, "Like a knife is pulling out of my liver."

Trotsky's Garden

TROTSKY IS WRITING. He will mention his love of life and his unqualified faith in dialectical materialism. He will mention Natasha, the strip of green outside his window, his invincible atheism, and he will contemplate his death. It is morning. Trotsky sits at his wooden desk. He looks at letters and a blotter. The Mexican sun burns in the green outside his window, just opened by Natasha. Trotsky notices. Natasha and the green slide into his writing. A man will strike Trotsky in the head with a pickax. Trotsky's sons—murdered—are mentioned in the writing. From Russia to Mexico, friends, secretaries, and bodyguards—murdered—are mentioned in the writing. In Berlin, where he sent her for psychoanalysis, his daughter killed herself. The pen does not cease or grovel in individuals. Trotsky will mention his faith in dialectical materialism, his faith in meaning. His mother suffered difficulties in reading; she crouched over novels and said, "Beta, alpha . . ." Trotsky says:

> If I could begin all over, I would try to avoid this or that mistake, but the main course of my life would

remain unchanged. I shall die a proletarian revolu-
tionist, a Marxist, a dialectical materialist.

Dialectical materialism, in the heat of the day,
draws a pickax from its raincoat. Some say "rusty
ax." Others say "ice pick." Trotsky himself noticed
nothing—it descended from behind—but he will
bite the assassin's hand. He is writing that if he
lived again, he would avoid mistakes. The sun, as it
did yesterday and will tomorrow, is shining.
Trotsky loves the green outside his window and
flourishes it in his writing. We shout, "O.K.,
Trotsky, no time for poems." He cannot hear us.
His poem is a march of corpses, the din is terrific.
Feet are beating in his writing. The sun is in the
green in his writing. Sedova, the aristocrat, lifts her
elbow for photographers. "See? A bullet made that
ugly scratch. My old man isn't nobody. Yesterday
they machine-gunned our bedroom." She means,
From revolution to Mexico, Trotsky is pursued by
his inventions. Trotsky himself says that he put the
idea of exile into the ear of Stalin's spy; hence, into
the mind of Stalin. In effect, Trotsky exiled Trotsky
and machine-gunned his bedroom. Now, writing
that one cannot be reborn until one is dead—and
look: it sits beside him with a raincoat and pickax.
It makes nervous conversation about alphabetical

materialism. Suddenly Trotsky is fighting, not writing. Blood runs into his eyes. Nevertheless, he catches the personal fact. Who said Lenin is morally repulsive, and Stalin is a savage who hates ideas, and Parvus is a fat, fleshy bulldog head? Trotsky said these things. Now the assassin's hand is in his teeth. With fury of intimacy, Trotsky bites. This hand wanted to remind him of something. But what? On the wall outside, the guards carry rifles and binoculars. They are gossiping in the sun when Trotsky screams. They see him standing in the window, bleeding and blind, a figure of history. "What?" he screams. The assassin is behind him, bent, sobbing like a child as he sucks his mutilated hand. The guards are running on the wall with their rifles and binoculars. Freud lights a cigar and contemplates this tableau. He says, "Trotsky and I were neighbors in Vienna." Trotsky admired Freud. He sent him his best daughter. Now Trotsky shouts in the window: "What does it mean? Such heat. In such heat a raincoat . . ." Trotsky flings toward his wooden desk. He needs only seconds to write: "On hot days in Mexico beware of raincoats."

Annabella's Hat

1

THE BUTLER SAYS, "Lord Byron jumped out
of the carriage and walked away." Annabella appeared next. The butler says, "The bride alighted,
and came up the steps alone, her countenance and
frame agonized and listless with evident horror and
despair." A scarf, twisted about her head, was
bunched up in imitation of a hat. Others report the
arrival, among them Lord Byron. His memoirs were
burned. One who read them claims Lord Byron took
Annabella before dinner. They withdrew after dinner and lay in a four-poster bed near a fireplace.
The crimson curtains of the bed, quickened by
firelight, made flickering blood-colored walls. Lord
Byron imagined himself within the membranes of a
giant stomach. "I am in hell," he screamed. Annabella crept downstairs, hid in the kitchen, and later
begged medical advice. Assured that Lord Byron
was mysterious, not mad, she hired investigative
agents. A year passes. The incontinent Lord Byron
flees to the Continent. His affair with his sister,
consummated before the marriage, is being noised
about. People cut him at parties. He flees; soon

thereafter, dies in Greece. Annabella's agents rush into the room. Lord Byron's servant—a bad-tempered man named Fletcher—draws his sabre, but they beat him unconscious and rip the boot from Lord Byron's crippled foot. They saw a hoof of great beauty, subtly united with the fetlock. The memoirs—where Lord Byron mentioned it—were burned at Annabella's insistence. Now, sufficient to say, in the mass of Byroniana—letters, scholarship, gossip—no extended reference to his hoof exists.

2

LORD BYRON published amazing poems. He had sexual union with his sister. Then came the wedding. Afterward, with Annabella and her maid, he rode forty miles from Seaham Church to Halnaby Hall, where he honeymooned. It is said the day was cold and Lord Byron despised the cold, but nothing is reported as to where he sat in the car-riage—beside Annabella or beside the maid, or if Annabella sat between, with the meat and bags and wine opposed. Fletcher, a sullen lout, refused to say a word. He galloped behind the carriage. It isn't known if the maid was acquainted with Lord Byron, or if they sat as strangers pressed, he by she, at turns in the road. Reported then, as here reported, Lord Byron was cold. Annabella's head, round as an Esquimau's, was conservative of temperature. It is known that Lord Byron's head, examined the previous year by the craniologist Spurzheim, was a structure of antithetical dispositions. The rest is inevitable. Indifferent to cold or hot—by nature, virtuous—the Annabella head through intimate contiguity with the crippled, incestuous bisexual caused him to feel dialectically cold, Satanic, probably squashed by the maid. It is rumored that he began shrieking, then stamping the carriage floor viciously with his hoof.

I Would Have Saved

Them If I Could

Giving Notice

A FEW DAYS PRIOR to the event, my cousin said, "I'm not going through with it. Call off the bar mitzvah." My uncle said, "You're crazy." My aunt said, "I think so." He'd already reserved the banquet hall, said my uncle, with a big deposit; already paid the rabbis, the caterers, the orchestra. Flying in from everywhere in the Americas and Canada were relatives and friends. My aunt said, "Deposit. Relatives." My cousin said, "Do I know the meaning of even ten Hebrew words? Is the bar mitzvah a Jewish ceremony? Do I believe in God?" My aunt said, "Get serious." My uncle said, "Shut up. The crazy is talking to me." My aunt said, "You too must be crazy." My cousin said, "Call it off." My uncle said, "I listened. Now you listen. When the anti-Semites come to kill your mother, will it be nice to say you aren't a bar mitzvah? Don't you want to be counted?" My cousin pulled open his shirt. "Look," he cried. My aunt said, "I can't talk so I can't look." "Look," he screamed. Green, iridescent Stars of David had grown from his nipples. My uncle collapsed on the wall-to-wall carpet. Looking, my aunt said, "I can't talk so I refuse to look at your crazy tits." That night my uncle sent telegrams throughout the Western Hemisphere. He explained, with regrets, that his son didn't believe in God, so the bar mitzvah was canceled. Then he pulled my cousin's five-hundred-dollar racing bike into the driveway, mangled the handlebars, kicked out the spokes, and left it for the neighborhood to notice.

A Suspected Jew

JAROMIR HLADÍK is suspected of being a Jew, imprisoned by the Gestapo, sentenced to death. In his prison cell, despite terror and confusion, he becomes ecstatic, then indistinguishable from his ecstasy. He is, in short, an ecstasy—the incarnation of a metaphysical state. Borges wrote this story. He calls it "The Secret Miracle." Whatever you call it, says Gramsci, it exemplifies the ideological hegemony of the ruling class. In the mediating figure, Jaromir Hladík, absolute misery translates into the consolations of redemptive

esthesis. It follows, then, the Gestapo, an organiza-
tion of death, gives birth to "The Ecstatic Hladík"—
or, to be precise, "The Secret Miracle." Borges,
master of controlled estrangement, makes it impossible to feel that Jaromir Hladík—say, a suspected
Jew of average height, with bad teeth, gray hair,
nervous cough, tinted spectacles, delicate fingers,
gentle musical voice—physically and exactly dis-
integrates (as intimated in the final sentences)
between a hard stone wall and the impact of
specific bullets.

The Subject at the Vanishing Point

MY GRANDFATHER—less than average
height—had bad teeth, gray hair, nervous cough,
tinted spectacles, delicate fingers, and a gentle
musical voice. To appear confident and authentic,
worthy of attention by clerks in the visa office, he
memorized the required information—his mother's
maiden name, the addresses of relatives in America

—and, walking down the street, he felt constantly in his coat pockets to be sure that he had photos of himself, wife, daughter, enough money for the required bribes, and the necessary papers—documents from America, passports, birth certificates, and an essay by himself in praise of Poland—when a pogrom started. Doors and windows slammed shut. The robots were coming. Alone in a strange street, he couldn't tell which way to go. At every corner was death. Suddenly—for good or ill isn't known—somebody flung him into a cellar. Others died. He, bleeding and semiconscious, hidden in a cellar, survived the pogrom. That day he didn't get a visa to leave Poland. He was a tailor—short, thin-boned. Even in a winter coat, easy to fling. He crawled amid rats and dirt, collecting his papers. When night came and Poland lay snoring in the street, he climbed out of the cellar and ran home. Wife and daughter ministered to his wounds. All thanked God that he was alive. But it was too late to get a visa. The Nazis came with the meaning of history—what flings you into a cellar saves you for bullets. I don't say, in the historical dialectic, individual life reduces to hideous idiocy. I'm talking about my grandfather, my grandmother, and my aunt. It seems to me, in the dialectic, individual life reduces not even to hideous idiocy.

Material Circumstances

His IDEA ABOUT LABOR POWER came to him while he strode back and forth in his room in Paris and smoked cigarettes. Indeed, striding back and forth, he smoked cigarettes, but striding, smoking, whistling, etc., are contingent activities. What *matters* is the stage of development in the class struggle when it is possible for a person to think seriously—to have an idea—about labor power. Certainly, in Paris, Karl Marx strode, for example, smoking cigarettes. Now and then, he strode to the window, pushed it open to free the room of smoke and listen for developments. But the precisely particular determinants of consciousness, within the class struggle, are material circumstances. Intuitively, perhaps, Karl Marx felt the burden of determined consciousness in the black, thick hair thrusting from the top of his head like implications and slithering down his chest and back to converge at his crotch, like a conclusion. But, even scrutinizing the hair beneath his fingernails (very like the historical grain in wood), he detected nothing beyond

mute, inexorable flux until—striding, smoking—
he pushed open his window and noticed Monsieur
Grandbouche, his landlord, a figure of bourgeois
pieties, who shouted, "When will you pay the rent,
my hairball?" Karl Marx strode back and forth and
smoked. *La question* Grandbouche burned in his
roots, like the residue of a summer rainstorm,
quickening the dialectical material of his struggling
circumstances. Hair twisted from his ears and
whistling nostrils. Angry messages. An idea was
occurring. Indeterminable millions would die. Indeterminable millions would eat. Thus, a Parisian
landlord, frightened by a smoky blotch in the
window, shouted a pathetic joke in the spirit of
nervous conviviality, and, as a result, his descen-
dants would be torn to pieces, for he'd epitomized
material circumstances by shouting—across gen-
erations of Grandbouche—an idea, intensified by
repercussions, echoed in concussions of Marxian
canons, tearing fascist ligament even in the jungles
of the east. *Voilà*, implicit in a landlord's shout is
the death rattle of his children's children.

Business Life

My UNCLE invested his money in a beauty parlor, began to make a little profit—and the union representative came. My uncle promised to hire union workers soon as the mortgage was paid. Pickets arrived. Back and forth with their signs in front of the beauty parlor. My uncle brought them coffee. They talked about their troubles. A picketer didn't have a soft job. Long apprenticeship; pay wasn't good; and morning to evening, march, march, march, screaming insults at my uncle's customers. The signs didn't look heavy, but try to carry one all day. My uncle agreed: a sign is heavy. Anyhow, business improved. After a while the union bombed the beauty parlor, set fire to my uncle's car, and beat up my aunt. This was reported in the newspaper. Business became much better. My uncle negotiated for a second beauty parlor. One afternoon a picketer leaned against the window of the beauty parlor and lit a cigarette. My uncle started to phone the union, but he hadn't forgotten his life in Russia, his hatred of informers. He put down the phone. The image of that man— slouched against the window, smoking, not carrying the picket sign so that people could read it— seethed in my uncle like moral poison. He soon developed a chronic stomach disturbance. Next came ulcers, doctors, hospitals—all the miseries of a life in business.

Literary Criticism

PHOTOGRAPHS OF SUSPECTED JEWS—men, women, children with hair, teeth, etc.—are available in great sufficiency. If you demand one, either you hate, or do not understand, Borges's critical point, which is that any reader knows stories of this exquisitely general kind. Besides, Borges made his story not from photographable reality—your Polish relatives whose undernourished kosher height never exceeded five feet six inches—but from a stupid story called "The Occurrence at Owl Creek Bridge." My aunt, a schoolgirl, was bleeding on the ground with her mother and father in Brest Litovsk.

Shrubless Crags

The Prisoner of Chillon, by Lord Byron, isn't essentially different from "The Secret Miracle." It too is about a condemned prisoner who becomes ecstatic. Suddenly, after years in a dungeon, Bonnivard transcends his mortality:

> What next befell me then and there
>   I know not well—I never knew—
> First came the loss of light, and air,
>   And then of darkness too:
> I had no thought, no feeling—none—
> Among the stones I stood a stone,
> And was, scarce conscious what I wist,
> As shrubless crags within the mist;
> For all was blank, and bleak, and grey;
> It was not night—it was not day;
> It was not even the dungeon-light,
> So hateful to my heavy sight,
> But vacancy absorbing space,
> And fixedness—without a place.

Like Hladík, in a state of intensified absence, he is a presence.

Leonard Michaels

Song

BYRONIC ROMANTICISM entered the Russian soul, at the deepest level, as evidenced in the beloved folk song, "Oi yoi, the shrubless crags."

Blossoms

METAPHYSICAL POSSIBILITIES—Hladík, Bonnivard—as inherent in the world, are appreciated by Wordsworth when he focuses on shrubless crags and imagines them spiritual entities, theoretical men who neither live nor die. They hover in the mist of universal mind, or the moods of finitude. In a snowstorm outside Smolensk, fighting the Nazis, my uncle was hit in the head by shrapnel, carried to a hospital, and dropped in the dead ward. That night a Jewish woman, who was

a surgeon and colonel in the Russian army, discovered him when she left the operating room and,
to smoke a cigarette, retreated to the dead ward. A
vague moan, "Mama," reached her from shadowy
rows of corpses. She ordered a search. Nurses running down the rows, pressing back eyelids, listening at mouth holes, located my uncle. The body
wasn't dead; more you couldn't say. The surgeon
stepped on her cigarette. "I'll operate." My uncle
lived, a hero of the people, guaranteed every right
of Russian citizenship. At his first opportunity he
fled, walking from Russia to Italy through the confusion of ruined cities; stealing by night across the
borders of Poland, Czechoslovakia, Rumania, and
Austria; starving, pursued by dogs and police, and
always repeating to himself the address of his sister
in lower Manhattan. When he got to America he
struggled for years, with little English and great
anxiety, to make money. Today he owns race tracks
and a chain of beauty parlors. He drives a Lincoln
Continental. Though he speaks six languages, he
isn't much of a conversationalist, but likes a good
joke, especially if it comes from life—how, for
example, during a Chinese dinner, his brother-in-
law's appendix ruptured. Both his sons are doctors
and drive Jaguars. He reminds them that his life

was saved by a woman less than five feet tall who, during the battle of Smolensk, performed miraculous surgery while standing on ammunition boxes. It could seem, now that he's a big shot, he gives lessons in humility. But how else to defend himself against happiness? He sees terrifying vulnerability in the blossoms of *nachas*.

The Screams of Children

THE NEW TESTAMENT is the best condemned-prisoner story. Jesus, a "suspected" Jew, sublimates at the deadly moment. In two ways, then, he is like Jaromir Hladík. Insofar as the Gestapo gives birth to the ecstatic Hladík, he and Jesus are similar in yet another way. Both are victims of parental ambivalence, which tends to give birth to death. One could savor distinctions here, but the prophetic Kafka hurries me away: humanity, he says, is the growth of death force. For reasons of discretion the trains rolled before dawn, routed through the outskirts of Prague. Nevertheless, you could hear the screams of children.

Heraclitus, Hegel, Giacometti, Nietzsche, Wordsworth, Stevens

NOT CONSIDERED from the point of view of children, parental ambivalence is a sentimental version of the much admired, familiar principle of destructive generation. According to Heraclitus and Hegel, it is applicable to everything. The Heraclitean dialectic is terse, impetuous, compulsively reiterated, and may be observed in the beautiful statues of Giacometti. Hegel's restatement is logical, passionate, exfoliate, and tremendous. Despite efforts by Nietzsche, it presently sits on Heraclitus like the buttocks of Clio, squeezing mind and world into one. Wordsworth manages the same—tactfully, however—urging mind and world into lyrical lament:

> A slumber did my spirit seal;
>   I had no human fears:
> She seemed a thing that could not feel
>   The touch of earthly years.

No motion has she now, no force;
  She neither hears nor sees;
  Rolled round in earth's diurnal course,
    With rocks, and stones, and trees.

With rocks and stones, "she"—an intensified absence—is a presence. In the negation of negation, she is. So are Hladík, Bonnivard, and Jesus. My grandfather was a tailor in Brest Litovsk. He vanished. Wallace Stevens says, "Death is the mother of beauty."

Alienation

IN HIS ESSAY "On the Jewish Question," written in exile, Karl Marx—an alienated Jew assuming the voice of a Hegelienated Jew—says, "Money is the jealous god of Israel." He means, by this oblique smear, the Virgin is a prostitute, her child is capitalism. Hence, it is Jesus—not the exiled Karl Marx—who objectifies alienation. And why not? The life of Jesus, described early and late by the absence of his father, is nothing less than the negation of negation. Marx never gives the least attention to the journey of the Magi, the mystery on the bestial floor, or the ultimate figure of Jesus in the excruciating pictorial epitome. For an execution Roman-style—with three prisoners and ritual para-phernalia—there is Lord Byron's letter.

Lord Byron's Letter

"The day before I left Rome I saw three robbers guillotined. The ceremony—including the *masqued* priests; the half-naked executioners; the bandaged criminals; the black Christ and his banner; the scaffold; the soldiery; the slow procession, and the quick rattle and heavy fall of the axe; the splash of the blood, and the ghastliness of the exposed heads—is altogether more impressive than the vulgar and ungentlemanly dirty 'new drop' and dog-like agony of infliction upon the sufferers of the English sentence. Two of these men behaved calmly enough, but the first of the three died with great terror and reluctance. What was very horrible, he would not lie down; then his neck was too large for the aperture, and the priest was obliged to drown his exclamations by still louder exhortations.

The head was off before the eye could trace the blow; but from an attempt to draw back the head, notwithstanding it was held forward by the hair, the first head was cut off close to the ears: the other two were taken off more cleanly. It is better than the oriental way, and (I should think) than the axe of our ancestors. The pain seems little, and yet the effect to the spectator, and the preparation to the criminal, is very striking and chilling. The first turned me quite hot and thirsty, and made me shake so that I could hardly hold the opera-glass (I was close, but was determined to see, as one should see every thing, once, with attention); the second and third (which shows how dreadfully soon things grow indifferent), I am ashamed to say, had no effect on me as a horror, though I would have saved them if I could."

Species Being

CASUAL PRECISION, lucidity, complexity of nuance, smooth coherent speed. I admire the phrase "great terror and reluctance." It makes the prisoner's interior reality and his exterior—or social —reality simultaneous. Surely he felt more than reluctance. But the word stands in contrast to "great terror" and thus acquires the specifically social quality of great terror suffered by an individual at the center of public drama. He could collapse and dissolve into his great terror, but doesn't. Nor does he become ecstatic. Instead, sensitive to the crowd, he tries to join it by conveying an idea of himself—as also watching, like the crowd, a man who is about to get his head chopped off, who is in great terror and who—reluctantly—is himself. He owes the crowd his head. He knows the crowd will have his head. The crowd didn't go to the trouble of gathering itself around him for nothing. He wants to indicate that he is not the sort who is indifferent to what the crowd wants, but, after all, it is his head it wants. Of course he is in no position not to provide it. The crowd sees that he has brought it with him. He would like, just the same, to suggest that he is "reluctant" to do so. At the last instant, he loses poise and pulls back. The result is a messy chop, a bad show. Ethics and aesthetics are inextricable. All this, and much more, is intimated in Byron's letter. Though it is infected, slightly, by ironical preciosity, the letter was written to somebody; therefore, like the prisoner, it participates in a consciousness other than its own; by attitudinizing, it suggests that it sees itself. This is Byron's concession to society; it is justified by his honesty—the childlike, high-spirited allegiance to the facts of the occasion inside and outside *his* head. Compared to the sneering, sarcastic, bludgeoning verbosity of Karl Marx, who walked in Paris, it isn't easy to believe the latter's idea of humanity as social essence is either witty or attractive.

Dostoevsky

IN DOSTOEVSKY'S STORY, a condemned prisoner—at the penultimate instant before a firing squad—is reprieved by the tsar. Dostoevsky says it was his own experience. The reprieve was announced, he says, and the firing squad—not the prisoner Dostoevsky—sublimated. What follows? In life and art at once, the tsar is a champion of imaginative forms. For condemned prisoners— which is all of us—the tsar, a true aristocrat, is godlike in his manifestations. Astonishing, arbitrary, inscrutable. More evil than good—but thus are we saved. From above! Of course, in historical fact the tsar and his family were slaughtered. Trotsky considered this "action" indispensable.

Stalin's considerations, regarding Trotsky and his
family, were identical. It is impossible to live with
or without fictions.

) *why?*
so

The Night
I Became a Marxist

I HEARD A VOICE, turned, saw nobody,
walked on, heard the voice again, but didn't turn.
Nobody would be there. Or somebody would. In
either case—very frightened—I walked faster,
stiffened back and neck, expecting a blow, anxious
to swivel about, but not doing it until I could no
longer, and, walking quickly, stiffly, swiveling to
look back, walk on, I noticed street lamps were
smashed, blackness took sections of everything,
signs were unreadable, windows glossy blotches,
doorways like sighs issuing from unimaginable in-
teriors. I felt absolutely outside, savage, and I'd
have begun running, but there was the park, the
streets beyond. I continued to walk, swivel, walk,
saving power, holding self—and then, hearing it,
whirled, dropped into a crouch, legs wide, fists
raised. I'd have seen nothing, nobody, but—

crouched low—realized, suddenly, I was face to face with it, shorter than a midget, speaking mouth, teeth like knives: "Always having fun, aren't you? Night after night, dancing, drinking, fucking. Fun, fun, fun."

His guilty conscience embodied in one nightmarish moment?

Conclusion

LONG BEFORE ruling-class, ideological superstructures, there were myths describing ecstasies like those of Jaromir Hladík and Jesus. Nymphs and beautiful boys, fleeing murderous gods, were always sublimating into flowers, trees, rivers, heavenly constellations, etc. The earliest stories, then, already convey an exhilarating apprehension of the world as incessantly created of incessant death. Nothing changes. Stories, myths, ideologies, flowers, rivers, heavenly constellations are the phonemes of a mysterious logos; and the lights of our cultural memory, as upon the surface of black primeval water, flicker and slide into innumerable qualifications. But Jaromir Hladík, among substantial millions, is dead. From a certain point of view, none of this shit matters any more.

A refusal to embrace his own consoling theme?

[138]

Hello Jack

J ACK PHONED.

I said hello Jack.

He said he was going to the hospital.

I said all right I'll go with you.

I asked if I should phone his wife. They weren't living together.

He said he wanted me to know where he was. He didn't want me to do anything.

I said you're the boss. What's wrong? I made my voice little.

He yelled let's not talk about it. I'm in the hospital.

I said you said that you had to go to the hospital. Little words. Cheepee cheepee cheepee. His wife couldn't stand him. I knew plenty.

I said hello Jack and rushed to the hospital.

I had a bad foot. Every step was a wolf bite.

But Jack was in the hospital. He was the boss.

Jack phoned so I said hello taxicab. He'd do the same for me. We were old friends from Novgorod. Nothing to think about.

Taxi. Taxi.

In the hospital I noticed everyone was dead. Then a nurse was walking. I yelled rooms rooms rooms.

She said she personally didn't build the hospital.

I said so where's Jack?

She said he was in a room with another man.

In a hall I was running.

I saw Jack. Compared to the other man, Jack was Mr. Universe. What the Mongolians did to one grandmother the Germans did to the other. They made a big blond Chinese Jew. His wife hated him. She was from Budapest. I didn't say anything.

What's with that man I said. I limped to a chair and took the shoe off my bad foot. The other man was blankets up to a face the color of chicken fat. His eyes were sticking out like swords.

Jack said the man was recovering from pneumonia. I didn't say anything.

If you ask me that man finished recovering I said. I put my shoe on Jack's bed.

Jack said what's the matter with your foot?

Nothing I said.

The man heard us. He said virus.

My foot was sweating.

Jack said virus is different from plain pneumonia.

I rubbed my foot. Poo I said. Open a window.

Jack said don't do anything. It's not important.

I said how much are they paying you to stay here? Stinks is not important?

I hopped to the window in one shoe and asked the virus I'm opening the window.

His eyes didn't move. They looked like a sign: BE QUIET. BE QUIET. Two killers, shining, pushing. He said virus.

I asked him again I'm opening this window so it will stop stinking.

He said virus.

A little snow came in. You couldn't notice. Like feathers. Nothing. It melted on the radiator. The virus didn't complain. Only a maniac would complain. The virus looked at the ceiling as if a movie was playing there. I looked too. I knew there was no movie on the ceiling but I looked. I was right. Jack was happier with the window open. Why not? He was a man with a friend. He began a speech why he was in the hospital.

He couldn't eat, he couldn't sleep. This. That. He fell down at work. In his stomach a pain. So his union sent him to the hospital.

Talk talk talk. I knew plenty.

I said I'm glad you want to talk.

He said is it wrong to talk?

I said tell me if what you have is serious and forgive me for laughing. A friend can laugh.

He said you think it's not serious?

I said to you serious is to the world ridiculous. Sure an enemy wouldn't laugh. He doesn't care so he can care. You have no sense of proportion. I rubbed my foot.

The other man said virus.

Jack said nobody told him not to talk.

I said maybe you would like to sing.

He began to sing. Ya-ya-ya.

The man said virus.

Me too. Ya-ya-ya.

All of a sudden the virus pushes his blankets on the floor and gets out of bed. His gown was pinched in his behind. His legs were bones, his face green. Like a tomato. I thought he was a tomato not a virus. He walked out of the room.

We stopped singing.

I said he went to the toilet.

Jack said a toilet is behind the door over there. He didn't go to the toilet.

I said how do you know? Maybe he doesn't like that toilet.

Jack said he didn't go to the toilet.

I said he'll be back in a minute. He went to

another toilet because he didn't want us to hear him make a tinkle.

Jack said he didn't go to any toilet.

I said all right. Then he recovered. Why should he pay another penny? He recovered. Stop the clock. A motel is cheaper. I noticed I had a headache.

Jack gave me a face like Genghis Kahn. A rock with eye slits. I could see the tomato was my fault. I could see it in the rock.

I said I know how it is Jack. You come in with trouble and they put you with a virus. Look at my foot. Is that sweat Jack? It's sweat believe me. Jack's wife hated him. A small skinny from night school. Hair and pimples.

She used to read to him from Goethe. He couldn't understand a word so they got married. When Jack had a hard-on she would vomit. He called her The Stomach. He used to say I'm going home now to The Stomach. I knew plenty. I said what do you say about my foot?

He said he phoned me so I would walk on my rotten foot. Then he grabbed my shoe and went to the window. A guy like him makes life meaningless.

Jack I said it was a shoe. You should throw

Goethe out the window. Maybe you're in the Mongolian mood to throw my other shoe out the window? I slapped it on his bed.

He threw it out the window.

How about this lamp I said.

Out the window.

These blankets you want to keep?

Out the window.

I said this is too big don't even look at it.

For a Chinese Jew the mattress was no trouble.

A nurse came in when I was pulling Jack's bed toward the window. She started hitting and scratching me. Jack knocked her down with a punch. I jumped on her face. Jack put his tongue in her wallet, then me, then we pushed the bed out the window.

We were singing ya-ya-ya when nurses and doctors from all over the hospital came in. Why not? How often do schmucks see a friendship?

I walked home without a shoe. Not one shoe. I begged myself to take a taxi. It's cold. It's snowing. Take a taxi. But I refused. No taxi. For proof I yelled taxi taxi. It stopped. Drive into a wall I said.

The driver looked at me. I made a Jack face. He picked up a wrench. I could see he was a maniac. I was standing without shoes and a maniac was coming with a wrench. He could hit me in the foot. When he pushed open the door another taxi knocked it off.

It figures I yelled. But he was hitting the other driver with the wrench. In the snow I ran away. You'll get pneumonia I said.

I said I hope it's a virus.

Then I saw a phone booth and called Jack's wife.

She said hello.

I recognized her voice because it was so little and quiet. That's how she talked. Like a one-year-old.

I said hello Jack's wife?

She said yeah Jack's wife.

I said Jack is dead.

She said what who?

I said you're no good believe me. East Side hospital.

She was screaming with her little voice what who?

I didn't say anything. I said I'm hanging up. You think my foot isn't killing me? What do you care?

She screamed wait wait.

I said Jack's wife?

She screamed yeah yeah Jack's wife.

I said Jack's wife from Goethe?

She screamed yeah Jack's wife.

I said listen. Let another person talk sometimes.

She stopped screaming.

Are you listening I said.

She whispered yes yes.

Gloonk I hung up.

That night Genghis Kahn and The Stomach
were together. I didn't say anything. I went home
and put my foot in the toilet bowl and flushed the
water. Who needs a hospital? Or a small skinny
from Budapest? Not for me. A friend calls and I
said hello Jack. I also have a toilet bowl. It sucks
my foot and soon it feels better. At night I knock
over the garbage bag under the sink so in the dark I
listen to them eat. The rats are happy. I'm happy. I
yell sleep. It comes like a taxicab.

Some Laughed

T. T. MANDELL locked his office door, then read letters from experts advising the press against publishing his book, *The Enduring Southey.* One letter was insulting, another expressed hatred. All agreed *The Enduring Southey*—"an examination of the life and writing of Robert Southey"— should not be published. Every letter was exceedingly personal and impeccably anonymous. Mandell, an assistant professor of rhetoric and communication art at Bronx Community State Extension, had hoped to win a permanent position at the college. But no published book, no job. In effect, the experts said T. T. Mandell should be fired. But in every negative lives a positive. Mandell could read the letters; Mandell could revise *The Enduring Southey.* Where he'd previously said "yes" or "no," he now said "perhaps yes," "perhaps no." Miss Nugent, the department secretary, retyped the manuscript, then mailed it to another press. It was rejected.

T. T. Mandell locked his office door, then read the letters. All different, yet one conclusion: *The*

Enduring Southey must not be published. Again there were insults: "To publish this book would represent an attack on the mind." Mandell wasn't troubled by insults. His life had been shaped by them. Two criticisms, however, were troubling:

> The introductory chapter is full of errors of fact and judgment, and the prose is like that of a foreigner who has no feeling for English and probably not much more for his indigenous bush tongue.

The other:

> The introductory chapter, where Mandell says he approaches Southey from the inside, is bad. The rest of the manuscript falls below its level.

Mandell realized, considering these criticisms, "Even experts can't agree." More important, a contradiction implied intellectual space. He could perhaps shoot *The Enduring Southey* through that space into publication. He corrected facts wherever he sensed them. With commas he jerked his style toward elegance. Because an expert had said the introductory chapter was best, Mandell put it last. Miss Nugent retyped, then mailed *The Enduring Southey* to another press. It was rejected.

T. T. Mandell locked his office door and thought: "I went to required schools, received required degrees, made changes required by experts. What then do they want?" It struck him: "A man can't be rejected. He can only reject himself." Thus he recovered will and, to the new criticisms, responded with vigorous compliance. He eradicated paragraphs and pages as if they contained nothing. Though he worried about leaving breaks in his argument, time was short. He could not say, when required to state his achievements, that for a long while he had been rewriting a book that he had been rewriting. Anyone could say that. Even a moron. The manuscript—retyped, mailed to a scholarly press called Injured Merit—was returned with a letter from an editor: "Chop Southey in half. Put in pictures."

T. T. Mandell locked his office door, removed his clothes; silently, he rolled on the floor.

To colleagues he showed the letter—not with pride but by the way, as if unsure of its tone. They said it urged, without committing the editor to a promise of publication, that Mandell rewrite and resubmit. He frowned, puckered, and said, "Hmmm." His colleagues stared. He himself wondered, fleetingly, if he wasn't a prick.

Mandell cut *The Enduring Southey* in half and inserted a photo of the library in the Bronx where he'd done research. Below the photo he wrote,

"Thanks." It occurred to him to insert a photo of himself. That might seem presumptuous, but he remembered scholarly books where the author's photo appeared—an old book on Southey, for example. In the library he found that book again, but no photo, only a drawing, and not of the author, but Southey. Mandell nearly cried. Instead, he laughed and told people. Some laughed.

The Enduring Southey was not resubmitted to Injured Merit. It had become too good. Miss Nugent mailed it to a university press. It was rejected.

T. T. Mandell locked his office door, then telephoned a number he had prepared for this eventuality. A moment later he spoke to a lawyer who specialized in outrage. Mandell told the lawyer what degrees he held and where he had been teaching, as an assistant professor, for several years, while he tried to fulfill the publication requirements of a scholar as well as the general institution of requirements as such. He spoke of his faith in the system. He said he wasn't a troublemaker or a critic of prevailing values but the author of a proper book rewritten according to the criticism of experts. There had been a time, Mandell said, when he wore sneakers to class, but upon noticing that no other faculty members wore sneakers, he quit doing so. There were other things of this nature, but, Man-

dell believed, the lawyer had the picture. The lawyer then explained: "Professor, there's no action in
this crap." Mandell read the letters, revised the
manuscript, threw out the photo. Miss Nugent retyped, mailed. *The Enduring Southey* was rejected.

T. T. Mandell locked his office door. As if from
the abyss of authenticity, a voice came: "It doesn't
matter if you're a nice guy." Mandell listened. The
voice continued: "I made the whale." Mandell felt
depressed—or deepened. In this mood, he made
revisions.

Miss Nugent now wore glasses and walked
faster. Leaving her typewriter to go pee, she always
glanced at her wristwatch as if to confirm her need.
She retyped *The Enduring Southey,* mailed it away
again, then again. Mandell's face had a greasy,
dissatisfied quality now, impossible to wash or
shave away, and his manner had gained spasmodic
vigor. Once he interrupted a conversation between
two colleagues, rushing up to their lunch table,
driving a bread knife into the Formica top, and
shouting, "You were talking about *Moby Dick,*
right?"

The Enduring Southey had been mailed away
for the last time. To Stuttgart. Miss Nugent believed the finest scholarly books were published
there. Mandell could afford no more rejections, cer-

tainly none that might take long in coming, but Miss Nugent felt *The Enduring Southey* was hers as much as his. She wanted the last rejection to come from the best. *The Enduring Southey* was accepted.

A VW mechanic in Mandell's neighborhood translated the letter for him. Mandell waved it at Miss Nugent and flung into a dance before her typewriter. She pummeled the keys and hissed, "Don't let them have it. Tell them to screw off." He gave her a look of terror and fled.

Der andauernde Southey was published. Mandell was given permanency. He mastered the ho-ho style of laughter and, at department meetings, said things like, "What fun." Discussing the book with students who, someday, would write one like it, he said it wrote itself. Nasty reviews appeared, but they were in German. Mandell was considered an expert and received manuscripts from university presses with requests for his opinion. His letters were always written with uncompromising and incisive hatred.

The Captain

HE SMILED AT HER. She smiled at him and ate dessert, her pinky so nicely hooked it tore my heart. Dessert was pear under chocolate and flaming brandy. It slipped from spoon to blubbery dissolution. When I tried to taste, I swallowed. Then came a flickering city of liqueurs. Then marijuana, a language green and gold popping around the table from mouth to mouth. Nothing went by me un-lipped. Nothing tasted. From course to course I'd swallowed textures, not tastes, like a cat gobbling kill. I'd eaten; I wanted to eat. Other guests flashed marvels achieved, readiness to die. Music from the drawing room—black, full of drum—summoned us to further pleasure. Actual blacks, stationed around the table, stiff and smug in tuxedos, gleamed con-summation. I assumed they'd pissed in our soup. Stanger smiled at Mildred. She at him. Above glass, silver, flowers, candles, and the ministrations of swift black hands, everyone at the table had smiled for the last two hours. Servants are the price ele-gance pays to pain. Alone, the Stangers couldn't have made this occasion for forty guests; not without threatening every institution upon which society stands. To that sentiment, I drank piss. A ritual initiation. I'd never been to such a dinner party, but I could tell it was first-rate. Teeth stabbed out of my ass to eat the chair. However, the meal was over. Stanger rose. His hand claimed my wife's lower back. They strolled to the drawing room, a sight flattering to me, the lovely valley of her back appreciated in his munificent hand. Yet it gave me a feeling I couldn't understand, act upon, or use. Like Hamlet's feeling in Elsinore. But this was no dingy, boozy castle in barbaric Denmark. This was Now Town, Sutton Place. Windows triangulated, above the East River, north to Welfare Island, south to the Statue of Liberty. I couldn't make a speech or kill. I did what I could. I tried not to look at them, not to see. I joined the other guests, wondering what brought them here. Did they all want jobs? During our interview, Stanger said, "Come to dinner, Mr. Liebowitz. On Bastille Day. We'll chat some more about the job." I arrived. He nodded at me, took Mildred's arm, then talked to her, no one else, and here I was, his dinner in my gut, his grass in my brain, talking to myself, thinking grass. How did you play this game? Like a delegate to my thinking, Mrs. Stanger swept boldly through the grass. "So, Mr. Liebowitz, you're interested in publishing," and she led me to a chair opposite hers. "You'll make a lovely publisher." Her shoes were gold, her dress was white material through which I couldn't tell if I couldn't see. Intimations of symmetry seesawed her voice. Slowly, precisely, she crossed her legs, sliding white skin beneath white, translucent membrane. Her shoe began winding in the air. I looked.

"You can have the shoe, Mr. Liebowitz. Are you a man who wants things?"

"Everyone must want your things, Mrs. Stanger."

And that's what I thought. Yet I had to beg Mildred to dress for this party, comb her hair, show me good girl in the aspect of sullen bitch:

"Do you *want* to walk so quickly, Phillip? Do you *want* to suppose Stanger won't give you the job if we're two minutes late? Is it thrilling to have people think you're out with some whore? Is that what you *want*? Take my arm, you bastard, or I don't go another step."

A savage ride on the IRT, then worse in the crosstown cab.

"Two bucks for a lousy cab. But if I need, really need, a pair of shoes, you throw a fit. Tomorrow, I buy shoes. Hear me?"

She hadn't wanted to go. I had wanted to rush. Stanger had nodded at me, taken her arm, and la-la—I looked—his hand was on her knee. Wanting not to go, she had a moral advantage. She could now blow him and lift a virtuous face: "Don't give me that jealous crap."

Mrs. Stanger, apparently, wanted symmetry. A social lady with a Viking face, symmetrical by instinct. The ghost of long bone figure, unexorcised by a life of such occasions, still fighting, giving good as it got. Perfect for Stanger. Why not for me? One thinks meat or languishes.

Her eyes were tiger-bronze. They looked at me; not across the room at them. She seemed to be saying, "Do you really want the job, Mr. Liebowitz?" And she was. Winding her shoe, stirring a golden pool of time. I had five seconds, perhaps, to seem not stupid. The mathematics of her face demanded speed and precision, answers in kind, not self-analysis. I clicked on the smarts:

Stanger wanted Mildred. His missus wanted me. I wanted the job. The question was, then: What could I get? The answer answered everything. If I couldn't get only what I wanted, I had to want what I could get, to get what I wanted. Things equal to the same equal one another.

"Do you really want the job, Mr. Liebowitz?"

I said, "Let's fuck."

She blinked and shook her head. She sighed.

I had been too quick, too smart. I shrugged like a man with nothing more to say, and looked across the room at them, sitting close together on a couch, talking. To express life's failure, I lifted a cigarette. Mrs. Stanger knocked it out of my mouth. "That's a social disease, Mr. Liebowitz." She stood up in a blur of dancing and a storm of jazz, turned, pushed through shuddering couples, and went around a corner, disappeared. Reappeared. Frowning at me. To my feet I leaped.

Down a hall in pursuit of her gliding back, feeling concentrated in crotch, monolithic shark with blood in its nose and no appetite for analysis. I'd read that eating is the final extension of touch and believed it. I also believed the reverse. Paintings, etchings, Chinese jugs, chairs, tables, sculptured metals whispered as they flashed by, "Beast, beast, beast." Right. Psychology and art were dead. I didn't understand my motives, but that didn't prove I had any. Does the moon have a motive? Aristotle says, "Love." All right, love. Later, with nothing at stake, I'd return to this hall and contemplate a jug, make excuses for love, recall the meal, the hideous smiling, how he didn't talk to me, how Mildred did. I'd argue, Between me and Mildred had loomed the shape of a foreign penis. His moon. My motive. I'd recall the job, my own penis, and I'd

Is Michaels, too, an enemy of Freud? Why?

raise the distinction between men and women. Men do what they have to do. A woman can do anything a man can do, but does she have to? Mrs. Stanger didn't have to open the door. I stepped through it into another world. The enemy of Freud, the son of Marx, Phillip Liebowitz. Plunging beyond analysis in the wake of a shark.

The walls bore guns, horsewhips, heads of gazelle, buffalo, giraffe, and photos of Stanger amid naked blacks and guns. Dead animals lay at his feet. Mrs. Stanger locked the door and turned with her shoes kicked off, standing shorter, flat-footed, loose in arm and shoulder, chin up to give me a level glance from slits. Her expression, face and body, said, "Go on, look, Mr. Liebowitz. I'm without my shoes and no less terrific." There was a dull lamp in a corner of the room. Its light mixed delicate oils for metal and a breath of leather. She advanced in it slowly, face darkening, slits shining. "Don't you dare fuck me." We used the back of a brown bear. Her face beneath mine, in a field of bristle, opened as she opened and opened. Her hands slid up my spine, then away, up through her hair. Rings clicked on bear teeth. She fingered the fangs until they were bloody, then lay still, silent, perfectly flat, showing the indifference to my glance and the perfect ease of a woman who is proud of her body. I dressed. When I stood over her, she said, "Poor me. See the boo-boo. Lick the boo-boo, Mr. Liebowitz." I kneeled. She fed me fingers. I licked. The mute choir of staring animals, fifty Mr. Stangers, naked blacks, instruments of pain and annihilation, dull light intimating the circles of her breasts and white shield of belly, thickening of hair and shadow at the conflation of thighs and greater labia, were in my mouth. I swallowed.

⌐ The party had mounted to its preclimactic moment, music booming, blacks winding about wheeling carts of ice, glasses, and bottles. I felt the general tension that precedes both success and failure. All could decline into scattered, desultory chit-chat or fly toward community. Two men, stripped to the waist, were fighting in a corner. Some guests made a circle about them. Most were dancing, or talking in groups. I returned to the chair I had been sitting in. Black hands fixed me a bourbon; yellow; kickling ice. Through it I watched Stanger and Mildred, the intense, wishy-washy figures of an erotic urn, evoking the prick of perpetuity. Blows, grunts, incoherent curses, spiced with squeals from spectators, filled gaps in the music. The ambience was dense, rude, various flow. Blacks in tuxedos; hard black rock; whites chatting, slugging, dancing the inventions of black kids in ghettos. To think was impossible. I couldn't have added two and two unless driven by hatred or an equivalent passion. I couldn't have read a paragraph of Austen or James unless I shrieked each word. Mrs. Stanger remained behind to wash. I had nothing to do but sit, feel the life, watch Stanger and Mildred, drink my bourbon. Then a big wild lady plopped into Mrs. Stanger's chair. Her dress was channeled to discover tits, her talk was electrified by topics of slick magazines—decadent New York, divorce, the problems so many had these days with kids. She mentioned grass raps, politics, syphilis, runaways, and said, "I used to play kissing games, but today a kid spots a hair on his crotch and runs out to fuck." She waited for my comment. I grinned agreement. Between her tits the stream of little hair was bleached. Her own kid, she said, making a bomb, had blown out his eye. "Blew it out," she sneered, as if amazed at his incompetence. My head shook sympathetically while inside—along with the tiger haunted by former ass and thigh—I added first-class eats, marijuana, servants, and the job, say twenty thousand. "Blew it out," she repeated, en-

couraging me to respond. I tried for a sexual-
philosophical tone. "There is nothing left not to do,
is there?" She looked puzzled and annoyed, as if,
despite blatant tits and endless mouth, she hated
double messages. "I mean, you know, make bombs.
Fuck. What have you." The men fighting had begun
to shout. One claimed the other had kicked him in
the balls, which was against the rules. Then the
blows were thicker and louder. Tits laughed,
slapped her hand lightly on my face, and gave it a
little push, the way one treats a naughty child.
Affectionate repudiation. "You're a gas," she said,
her hand lingering on my lips, but, sensing a prior
claim, she withdrew it. Mrs. Stanger had appeared
and stood looking down at us. I tried to keep the tits
sitting by turning my back slightly to Mrs. Stanger.
But the tits, unnerved, rose from the chair and
turned her ass to me, as though displaying another
pair of tits in departure. Mrs. Stanger reassumed
her chair. I leaned toward her in humble admiration and squeezed her thigh. "I wanna marijuana,
Mrs. Stanger."

"You can begin calling me Nell. Why do you
want a marijuana? Didn't you like fucking me?"

Her expression was imperious. Her voice was
irascible.

"I see no connection."

"There is one. Answer my question, Phillip. Didn't you like it?"

"I didn't like it, Nell."

"Are you being moral?"

"My only luxury."

"A luxury of poor, sad, uneducated people. I liked it very much. Perhaps you're more fussy than moral."

She made an amused eyebrow and leaned back in the theater of great class.

"I'm sure my husband may give you the job."

I forgot that she wheezed and didn't sweat right. She saw that in my face. Fresh color leaped into her bronze, as if to meet some gift I held. She was ready again. So was I, but I didn't move. I couldn't predict tomorrow's feelings if I allowed no forbearance. A man needn't be immoral to know that. He feels things. Her hand on mine. We stood up together. Pretending to dance, we drifted toward the zoo, both of us quivering with the nastiness of our exchange. Sobs issued from the corner. Blows persisted. She said, "One of those chaps is a plastic surgeon."

"Which?"

I asked the question in a quiet, natural voice, like hers, to seem as ready as she for anything, even conversational drivel. And I turned her slightly to face the corner. "Which one?"

"The bigger one. His name is Swoon. I'll introduce you, if you like. I've never seen him at a party where he doesn't fight."

"You've invited him here before?"

"God, yes. About fifty times. You and your wife are the only ones never here before. He killed a man in that corner. February. Yes, it was February."

"Curious name."

"Silly. I mean he killed him in February."

She kissed my cheek. Stanger and Mildred receded through hair, vapors of perfume, alcohol, and cigarettes, immobilized figures on the couch, begging for trouble. In the zoo I buggered Nell. She noticed smears, said, "Shit," and ran off to change.

Nothing definite had been said about the job, but I was doing all right. Swoon, on the other hand, was down, spinning on his back while the other man, with pointed shoes, kicked him in the face, skipped away, stopped, kicked him in the face again and skipped away. A lady with bulging eyes and tendons scoring her neck shouted, "Get up, Jack, get up. Get up, you fairy." Beyond the fight, through agitations of dancing couples, I saw his hand on her thigh. She offered semiparted lips, lick of bare leg, pure neck and arm, and inflexible attention to him. She was lovely all in all. To me, a stranger. I'd have fucked her myself, though the idea seemed unnatural. She was mother of my child, not lady of this glory. However unnatural, I wanted her and envied her. I wondered how long before I was homosexual by circumstance. "Didn't you want me to do it, Phillip?" That they hadn't once left the couch was proof they felt something. "I did it for your job."

"No lies. Just tell me if you liked it."

"He was revolting. An old man."

"That means you liked it."

Swoon suddenly seized the dancer's crotch and dragged himself up through seven or eight punches in the face. The move was brilliant and courageous. I found myself shouting, "Go, baby. Kill. Kill. Kill." A voice hissed into my ear, "Devil." In another dress, another degree of fresher, whiter person, Nell smiled, then pinched at my kidney, screwing the flesh until I thrust an elbow into her abdomen. I giggled and tried not to look at the fight or across the room at dirty Mildred. To my giggles, shifting, and lack of focus, Nell said, "The toilet is that way." I said, "Thanks," wondering if I had to piss. She smiled, and her smile deepened, taking knowledge of her devil into places she'd taken the man. She knew him, this devil: he had to piss. In fact he didn't, but he smiled, too, at her periodontal plastic, pink, low in the gleaming tooth. As I started away she grabbed my elbow.

"Tell me one thing."

The fighting and the music were loud. I gave her a steady, deaf look.

"I want you to tell me one thing before you go." She didn't stop smiling.

"It was all right, Nell."

"But?"

I waited to see what she made of nothing.

Her smile strained as if tugged by waters. "You'd like to beat me, wouldn't you? I think you'd like to beat me."

I winked.

The other man went down. Swoon was grinding a heel into his neck. People were cheering, calling his name. "Jack. Jack." That was love, waves of love. Nell clasped her hands on her breast and jumped up and down. "Oh, kill, kill," she said. "Make him be dead."

Like a child, a little girl. Yet her exquisite jumping epitomized the party, spoke for the fighting men, and the others, too, even the servants.

They served, danced, fought for the lady in white and gold, of the symmetrical face. The spot where she pinched me seemed to burn a message into my kidney. Her crowd wasn't made of phonies. Between desire and action they interposed no mask. Impulse didn't twist into perversion, into games. They were whole, straight, noble creatures, slave and master. To me, the challenge they represented left no alternatives. Maybe Stanger and Mildred had seen to that, but I was glad that I'd made the first deadly stroke, going to the zoo with Nell, killing Mildred as surely as Stanger killed giraffes. I imagined him on the veldt, amid naked blacks who hand him gun after gun, begging him to shoot straight as the giraffe charges. Great, but I'd buggered his wife. I'd wanted the job. Now, I could not *not* have it. Something definite would be said tonight. Yes or no. Either answer would be a comment on myself. Before the evening was over I'd be purged of irony. Made clean. Hired. Or a simple schmuck. I'd walked off in the direction indicated by Nell. My step was light. Too light, nearly wraithlike in the spacious, winding substance of this apartment. It made me feel weak and sick, the apartment, the creepy trivial way I walked in it. Like a man looking for his own pathetic step on a huge ship at sea. A man who has never seen or felt a high sea, never learned to walk its long surge, its remorseless drag and lunge. I needed this moment away from the blazing, loud incoherence of the crowded land, alone, out of sight, to practice walking. And my feelings, while practicing, were like those of a young captain in a novel by Conrad. First opportunity to command. He is alone, pacing the deck, getting a sense of himself. A storm is rising on the horizon. Members of the crew try to call it to his attention, but he has already noticed it, and seen through it to himself. He is sympathetic to their fears, yet more sympathetic to his own. Could I get at that sense of myself required by this storm? I notice it's a moral storm. The worst kind. The ship is fraught with goods meant for the best people. Could I bring it home intact? Was I the captain? I tried to walk right. One, two, three, six, fifteen . . . It wasn't easy to walk right. No prerequisite of honor is easy. I was afraid I might kick a jug, scratch a painting, the way I walked, like a crazy, spastic, stoned, drunken gawk. Not a captain. I might even fall off the whole fucking ship. But then I felt it begin: one, two, three, four . . . I was walking, and all right. I was the captain.

A hallway led to hallways, to rooms opening into rooms, a labyrinth, a weight of money, ac-

cumulating in vistas of paintings, etchings, hanging rugs, pewter, throbbing lacquers, silver, gold.
Touch these good things, I thought. Let sublimation
steel you. Touch. Let lech. Love any hole that feels.
I smacked a door, hands flat to spare me a broken
nose, and fell through onto my face. I looked up
moments later and saw a girl at a dressing table.
Her back was to me. She was brushing long brown
hair, like the household genie of serene indifference. She didn't seem to know or care that I lay
behind her on the floor, watching. She spoke:

"Please don't apologize for being late and
slamming through my door like the offensive pig
you happen to be. I much prefer your silence. Any
apology will make me exceedingly furious. I'm not
exceedingly furious now, Colin. So keep your
mouth shut. I suppose you haven't shaved, have
you? I won't hear your apologies. I won't hear your
voice."

She clapped the brush down. Her legs lashed
by my face, negligee flying, to the bed. Books and
papers were knocked off the bed. I stood. She flung
onto the bed, twisted onto her back, eyes shut, forehead writhing with contradiction. She gave a blind,
shrill order to the ceiling:

"Go on, Colin, you know what I want."

Lest he'd forgotten, her legs struck out, stiff, isoscelean. I saw voluted conch in wire tangle, the picture of her mind. The Colin in me rose, perked up like a rat, snout quivering, pointing at the answer to a question never asked. Life is this epitome. Red, tidal maw. Yawn. Aching exfoliant. Hole. I flicked light, shut door, three steps, and I straddled her neck. "Smells," she cried, and muddy flux dragged me, gripping my head, churning circles into the circles of her need, the cherished head which she recognized—"Who you?"—as not the right head. A good one nonetheless, already thinking how to apologize. She screeched and kicked. I pressed on to suggest the suction of feeling, but, thinking, thinking, I felt only ideas, tones, and tropes rise upon one another like waves, curling, crashing, failing to hold, sliding faster, faster down the beach to the seething, shapeless inane. Remember the job, I thought, and a hairy hemp ripped from my liver to my throat. I came at both ends simultaneously. Apology was impossible. I opted for vigor. "Fantastic," I cried, hoping thus to distract her with vigor. Also oblique flattery. She said, "Eeee," scrambling to one end of the bed, and me to the other, pleading, "Don't scream. I'm turning on the light." It discovered her biting the sheet. "Woo

woo woo," she said. I bent, pleading in the harm-
less posture of a dog at stool. "Didn't you like
it?" She twisted about to slap the night table. I expected a gun. She twisted back, glasses on her face,
big eyes, the tigerish mother apparent. "Say, you're
Nell Stanger's kid, aren't you?" My voice was eager,
genial. She screamed. I fled.

Streaming chair, rug, jug, I whipped into the
last hall, kicked into high for the heart-bursting
straightaway, and a person—shortish, bald, bow
tie, drink in chubby grip—was there, like the eter-
nal child who plays in the road before the speeding
Ferrari, or the peasant lifting slow, clotted, labori-
ous face to a thunder of horses and hounds, but this
particular incarnation of the common denominator
leaned toward a painting, touching, smelling, wal-
lowing in the color and texture of converging
neural streams which filled the airy delta between
himself and better life on the wall, and was un-
aware of me, running, whole man running, legs,
arms, head running, stomach, knees, balls running,
and he still savored the painted dream as he looked
up into the oncoming real, the drink warm in his
forgotten fist, all of him big, bigger in my eyes,
looking up with no intention, no expectation, and
before his eyebrows fully elevated, eyes fully

opened, and pulpy sluggish lip curled fully away from stained teeth, my hands struck his neck. Behind me was a faint thud. Empty rumble of a rolling glass.

I reentered the drawing room with expanded lungs. Heat in my eyes. Couples were still dancing, others sprawled. Nobody watched Swoon and the other man, lugubrious with exhaustion, flailing in slow arcs, rarely hitting. Rancid breath lay in the torpid, festering air. Screams came from the distance. No cigarette was put out or drink lowered. Between me and the couch, where Stanger and Mildred sat necking, there was a forest of shifting fashions, the black tuxedos and the clothing of the guests, pinks, greens, blues, and yellows crying out for pleasures of middle age. It hummed everywhere, omnivorous conversation of a dying party that insisted on living. Nell stepped out of it. "Let's dance." Her voice was grim, as if dancing were war, but it had an undercurrent of something more particular. Instantly, I became a dancing fool. She danced me off to the zoo and said it.

"Undress."

Her clothes were a heap of white, pink, and gold. She sprawled on the bear, its fangs encrusted, shining blood. Her limbs cast out in the languid shape of her mood, suggesting nets. Her voice was soft, yet coarse in tone. "Get it, Phillip. On the shelf in the closet."

Still in my shirt and tie I trotted to the closet to get it, whatever it was. On a shelf about chest high lay three hundred sausages, coiled in convoluted complications, a monster brain. A long gray iron chain. The prospect of such appetite suffused me with feelings of poverty, no education, and moral shock, but in one clean movement of self-disgust I laid on hands like he who knows. The chain chuckled as my fingers pierced its holes. I pulled. It came slowly, heavily, as each link stirred from sleep, and then too heavily, gaining speed, personal will, clamor, a raging snake of cannon balls pouring through my hands to bury my feet, shins, knees. Writhing, arms out, I was half man, half bonsai tree with impoverished roots, strangled in its springs, sucking denial. "I hate pain," I screamed. Nell bobbled up off the bear. She seized the chain, tugged. I pummeled the top of her head. For real, not in a sexual way. She said, "Quit that." I shouted sincerely, "I hate pain. I'll beat your head off," pummeling. She lugged; steady, patient strength; the motion of serious, honest work. In different conditions, I'd have considered it beautiful; her naked, multidimpled back, rippling, heaving spine

against iron. I beat the measure of her lugging into
her head and shouted my refrain. At last I fell free
and could properly convulse. She rolled onto me,
tried to soothe me with mothery tongue, breasts,
and holes, but something had happened to make
me unreceptive, inconsolable, as if my body, in
trauma, had shaken free of my mind, and now my
eyes, my flesh in every place retreated, fleeing
toward the murdered buffalo, gazelle, and giraffe.
"That," I gasped, "rub with that." She, too, seemed
unselved, brained. She rose, stumbling across the
room to grab the giraffe by the nostrils and tear it
off the wall. She returned, kneeled, rubbed its eyes
and great slop of lip carefully, gently, against my
face and neck, then back and forth between my
legs until I felt better. I dressed rapidly. She stared,
sitting on the floor beside the giraffe, a limp, naked,
stupid woman. I let myself think of her that way.
"Get dressed, woman." She crawled to the heap of
clothing and clawed out her underpants. I left for
the drawing room. Not once had I struck her in a
deliberate and evil way. I thought of that as I
limped down the hall. I felt myself ringing like a
bell that calls men from this world. For the first
time that evening, if not in my life, doing nothing,
I'd done tremendously. Though nothing definite
had been said, I knew the job was mine. It was in-

conceivable that it wasn't mine. I hadn't hit her. I hadn't even wanted to. In the force of not wanting, I'd made the job mine. This wasn't magical thinking. This was true; or the world was chaos and less than hell. Nevertheless, I was prepared to accept a word, a strong hint. I didn't need legal forms, a ten-page contract, sixteen carbons. I would approach Stanger now. The confrontation would be his chance to talk, not mine. I had the job. He had only, for his salvation, to confirm it, suggest an idea of wages per annum. My limp deepened. I deepened it. Hard, good lunge. Dragging foot. An arm hooked back for balance, for the feel of bad damage swinging itself, dragging, lunging down the hall. What rough beast? What rough beast, indeed.

Suddenly the hallway didn't look familiar. I'd taken a wrong turn, perhaps two, but there was a door. It had no knob, a swinging door. I shoved it wide. Something registered. Just as quickly, it was gone, wiped out, retrogressively unseen. I was back in the hall again, the door was shut. I was about to continue lunging on to the next door, the next turn, when I realized I'd fallen into my old ways, protecting myself, letting myself believe there were things one mustn't see. I'd been through that, I'd seen, transcended. I could see anything now, see it

squarely, name it with exactitude and indifference.
I shoved the door again. It opened on a brilliant
kitchen, a long counter with a tall, steel coffee urn.
I'd seen that. The black servant stood on the
counter beside the urn. That, too. Pissing into the
urn. Yes, yes; that, too. He wore sunglasses as if to
shield his eyes against the glare of his yam. "That's
offensive," I said, naming it. He shook his last drops
into the urn, hopped off the counter, zipped up, and
began putting cups and saucers on a tray. When he
finished he turned to me and said, "We're born
offensive, brother." He stepped toward me, hand
extended, palm up. "Give me some skin, brother."
The flat, gleaming opacity of his sunglasses seemed
menacing, but I lunged to meet him and drew my
palm down his. We locked thumbs, pressed fore-
arms and elbows together. He was all right, but
boiling in me now was a phrase for Mildred: "Don't
drink the coffee." I returned to the drawing room
with it, and in the weariness of this crowd, I felt it
dissolve into the quiet voice of a Britisher, like head
boy at a school for supersadists, fashioning mana-
gerial scum for the colonies: "Mildred, get your
coat." Terribly mild, yet the pitch of majestic will.
She and Stanger were locked, pretzled together,
still necking, his hand was plunged beneath her
dress, but she wiggled hard, slapped knees to-

gether, sprang up. Suddenly my wife! He sprang up behind her. There were people everywhere, some standing behind their couch, others sprawled at their feet, and yet only I could invade their privacy, only I had the power of invasion attributed ordinarily to voyeurs and God. The power against which society makes laws, or out of which it claims to draw them. Now there was stir all about the room. My power had spread, initiating small spasms, like a wind seen in the motion of trees. And Nell appeared, the hostess again, cooing good-nights and so-good-yous. She smiled at me in a frowning, quizzical, sad, not miserable way. I read her lips: "Coffee?" Thus encouraging me to stay a bit after the others. I smiled regrets and waved lyrical goodbye. From the depths, dimly, mechanically, came "*Eeee.*" Some of the guests who seemed to hear it tried to look worried.

We left the apartment with Dr. and Mrs. Swoon. Stanger walked us out to the elevator. Dr. Swoon was in his clothes again. Mrs. Swoon, it turned out, was the lady with the bulging eyes and violent neck. Swoon's face was splotched with pimento color and torn. Somewhere behind it he seemed to have withdrawn into a severe dignity. Mrs. Swoon chattered as if it had been she who'd

done the fighting and could find no way of contain-
ing its momentum. "You should have gone for the
eyes, Jack. Your plan was no good. It never is when
you don't listen to people. I mean, you use diagnosti-
cians, don't you, before you operate?" She turned to
me. "Two of them. Jack has two young doctors who
see the patient and tell Jack what to do. Awfully
clever, but their hands are made of shit, you know
what I mean? Jack operates. Of course, without
them, he couldn't tell the difference between an
asshole and an elbow. I mean, he'd have to consult
the nurses to find out which was which. But once
he knows, look out, look out, that's Jack Swoon,
king of fingers. Never uses a knife on nose jobs. Do
you, Jack?" He shook his head no. "Does them with
fingers and the heels of his palms. This is the heel.
See, this part. Gets it smack up against the nares
and grinds. Makes nice little ski jumps every time.
'I make the whole world Gentile,' says Jack. Personally, I think it leaves the holes too big, but that's
what folks want." Stanger chuckled and raised a
voice to obscure hers, and also the screaming, which
followed us out to the elevator. "Didn't somehow
find a chance to talk to you, Phillip, and get to know
you. But I haven't forgotten our interview." His
thumb ground the elevator button as if it were an
eyeball. "We'll get together soon. You must promise

me that." Sufficient, I thought. Enough said. He had
dark, penetrating eyes and a feeble mouth. His expression was overbred, full of difficulties, as if
something in his chemical history wasn't finished.
An animal, perhaps, still to shoot. His handshake
was tentative, trying to close on a good-humored
assurance. Mine was a quick, up-down fuck-you. "I
promise. Good night. Thanks." He nodded to Mildred and they said good night as the elevator door
opened. Then he shook hands with the Swoons. We
stepped into the elevator. As the door slid shut he
turned away. The door stuck, by the grace of *deus
ex machina,* just for an instant, to show Stanger
with the right buttock in his fist, pulled away from
its brother. An abstracted, habitual gesture, ex-
pressing long familiarity with pressures of his body.
He released slow, thoughtful gas, a final good night
to his guests in the elevator. The door shut. Mrs.
Swoon stared at it. Dr. Swoon's fiery face ripped
into a great smile. I glanced at Mildred. She
pinched her nose. Even thus, beautiful. The door
opened, we said good night to the Swoons. She took
my arm. We walked wildly, bumping hips. "I was
bored, bored, bored," she cried. "Do you hear me?
Bored. The screaming was worth it, maybe, but I
was bored. I hope you're happy about the job. You'd

have gotten it even if we stayed home. Probably a better salary, too. Did you know a man was almost beaten to death and another had a stroke while looking at a picture? I wish I'd seen that picture. Must have been very dirty, don't you think?"

"He named a figure?"

"You imagine I asked?"

"Of course you asked."

"Eleven and a half to start."

"Bullshit. How much?"

"He said his daughter, Naomi, wants to be an actress. He calls her Nimi. Maybe it was Ninny screaming, rehearsing some part."

"How much? Don't prattle."

"He said she has a neurological problem. Theater is so good for her. 'So good for Nimi,' he said. He meant she's a crazy loony, right?"

"Who cares? How much?"

"The wife is very good-looking, but sort of a dopey slut, wouldn't you say? Wouldn't you say that, Phillip? He's a weakling. I'm sure you'll like the job, Phillip. You know what he told me?"

"What did he tell you?"

"He told me he hates the sound of eating, even the sound he makes. So he has these big dinner parties, see? Are you limping, Phillip?"

"Yeah."

"And he's got a scheme for buying property on the moon. Because of the blacks, not to make money. He's in lumber and publishing. He doesn't need money. There's a family place in Connecticut, to which we've been invited, and another one in California. But the moon, man, is where it's really at. 'Nowhere else to go,' he said. 'What do you think NASA is all about? Space agency? No, sir. Surreal estate agency.' No blacks on the moon, Phillip. He thinks New York is finished. Phones don't work. Blacks everywhere. But he hires black servants. What do you think that means, Phillip? He wants to keep an eye on them? Please stop that limping and walk more quickly."

"What the hell does he mean by eleven and a half? I'm no typist."

"Stop crying. I can't stand the sight of you crying."

"I'm not crying."

"Yes, you are. I'm tired. Let's take a cab all the way home. We can afford it. He said twenty-five. With his paw on my ass, he says twenty-five. 'Twenty-five, dear.' Jealous? Mrs. Stanger digs you. You should fuck her or something, if you haven't already. I hate you."

"You acted badly."

"I'm sorry I acted badly. There's a cab. Kiss me. Tomorrow I'll buy three pairs of shoes."

I kissed her in the cab, then asked, "Did you like Stanger's paw on your ass?"

"I liked the way you told me to get my coat in front of everybody. But if you ever do that when we're with human beings, Phillip, I'll do something you won't forget. Twenty-five. Hee-hee."

"Yeah."

The cab went west to Third Avenue, then north, then west through Central Park. The trees, lacerated by lights, seemed to fly into the cab and about our heads. Mildred leaned back, giving herself to the trees and to me. Her pants tangled at the ankle, but I couldn't get it out of mind and up again for naked traffic until she whispered, sliding down to the floor, whispering "Twenty-five" into my crotch. "Kootchie-kootchie." At our place the driver waited, a head on a leather jacket, smoke sliding and twining up like hair from his invisible cigarette, and the whole cab shuddering in idle. His photo looked down at us in the back, smiling; Nunzio Salazar, machismo-fascismo moustache, number 999327, approves of it. Mildred's legs seemed to lift from my ribs like wings. She said, "Oh," and came. I was satisfied. A sentimental man prefers happiness to truth. I did prefer it. Her dear, lovely cheek on my shoulder as I fingered sticky leaves, peeling away singles for the fare, twice as many for the tip. Mildred jerked. "Don't be a fool. We live in this town." Half as many for the tip.